You Don't Scare Me

by John Farris from Tom Doherty Associates

★ forthcoming

You Don't Scare Me

JOHN FARRIS

FORGE

A Tom Doherty Associates Book
New York

This is a work of fiction. All of the characters, organizations, and events portrayed in this novel are either products of the author's imagination or are used fictitiously.

YOU DON'T SCARE ME

Copyright © 2007 by Penny Dreadful Ltd.

This book is printed on acid-free paper.

A Forge Book
Published by Tom Doherty Associates, LLC
175 Fifth Avenue
New York, NY 10010

www.tor-forge.com

Forge® is a registered trademark of Tom Doherty Associates, LLC.

Library of Congress Cataloging-in-Publication Data

Farris, John.
    You don't scare me / John Farris.—1st hardcover ed.
        p.   cm.
"A Tom Doherty Associates book."
ISBN-13: 978-0-312-85064-7
ISBN-10: 0-312-85064-6
    1. Women college students—Fiction. 2. Stepfathers—Fiction.
3. Georgia—Fiction. 4. New Haven (Conn.)—Fiction. I. Title.

PS3556.A777 Y68 2007
813'.54—dc22   2006102557

First Edition: April 2007

Printed in the United States of America

0   9   8   7   6   5   4   3   2   1

For Mary Ann.
Without you,
this book and a dozen others
would not have been written.

I watched you with all the light and
darkness I have.

—*George Sefaris,* Summer Solstice

What is mind? Doesn't matter. What is
matter? Never mind.

—*doggerel that first appeared in the*
British magazine Punch, *in slightly*
different form, about 1855

You Don't Scare Me

Chase
Jubilation County, Georgia.
Ten Years Ago.

The first time Mama brought Crow Tillman around to the house, about three weeks after she'd met him, it was clear she already was head-over-heels. He hugged her a lot and gave her little kisses that had her simpering and said how glad he was to finally meet us. Us being me and my brother Jimmy. This was October, and about three years to the day they'd put Daddy in the ground.

I didn't know what to think of Crow Tillman at first. Didn't much care for his name, that was for sure. "Crow." Wasn't short for anything, or if it was, he never said. That's the name went on their marriage license later on. Too soon to suit Jimmy and me.

Anyway, he was tall, maybe six-two. Raven hair that he wore like an Indian, combed straight back and down over his shirt collar. Thick enough that he didn't have to gel or spray it. Said he had Choctaw blood. No reason to doubt him. He was plenty good-looking. The black eye patch didn't detract from his looks. He was lean and looked strong. A sharp dresser except for a ratty Richard Petty–style rancher's straw with a couple kitchen matches stuck in the band. He wore starched pressed Wranglers and rattlesnake-skin boots. There were little gold chains across the insteps. He wore gold chains around his neck and three gold rings. Only one tat, unless there were others in places I'd never see. But that tattoo was scary.

What happened to your eye? I asked him right off.

Mama just took a deep breath and held it. But I'd always spoke exactly what was on my mind, and at fourteen I wasn't about to change.

Lost it when I was ridin bulls in the PBR, Crow said. Did I say he smiled a lot? Too much, I was thinking. People who smiled all the time, in my estimation, didn't have a lot of humor in them. As we all learned later, that went double for Crow.

And, as I heard later, he never was a bull rider. It was the point of a bowie knife in a bar fight that took out his eye.

That's the way we learned about Crow, too late to save any of us: bits and pieces, rumors vague and rumors far-fetched. But they were all Jimmy and me had to go on; he wasn't forthcoming about any aspect of his life.

What's the patch for? I said. Don't you have a glass eye?

Now Chase, Mama pleaded.

Crow's smile got bigger.

Surely do. Want a see it?

Jimmy and me both nodded. Mama halfway turned her back.

He raised up the patch. Now that was the damnedest sight I'd seen in a long while. Jimmy gasped.

It was a round glass eye; not much eyelid to cover it. So the eye just stared at you. The pupil was yellow. And on it, like a white scar, there was a bolt of lightning engraved.

I looked at Mama like, Get rid of him, *fast*. I mean what kind of man spends money on an eye like that? Same kind, I suppose, has a coiled rattlesnake tattooed on the back of his left hand. That moved like it was fixing to strike when he made a fist a certain way.

Mama looked anxious to get Crow out of the house now that the formalities were out of the way, go someplace where she could dote on him in private. I knew he had to be screwing her silly. Maybe I was only fourteen but I already knew how it went. I felt cold in the pit of my stomach thinking about that rattlesnake hand on her.

What kind a work do you do? I asked.

I own some properties, Crow Tillman said. Pays me a tidy sum.

If it hadn't dawned on me before this, I sure had him pegged now. What he really wanted with Mama, what he truly was looking for.

Turned out I was only half right.

Before they went on their way for a night of line dancing at Cowboys and then to whatever motel Crow was staying at, we had to go outside to see his new truck, then admire his damn dog that was tied in the truck bed. Tied for a good reason. It was a scruffy mean-looking cuss. Black and tan with a chow ruff and probably weighed close to eighty pounds.

What's his name?

Angel, Crow said, and laughed. Then he said, Angelpie's what ye call a three-chaw dog.

Yeah?

Meanin if he bites ye three times you're as good as dead. Then he called me honey. I hated for anybody to call me that.

Well I won't be too late, Mama said, and she got into the quad cab of Crow's Silverado first. Like she couldn't wait to separate Crow from us. Although he didn't appear to mind our company all that much. My company.

I was a little slow to catch on. Maybe because I was so upset with Mama and not knowing what I should or could do about her crush on him. I mean, *properties*! He wasn't but a cut above a drifter, and I already sensed he could be lowdown as snail shit from that signal in his good eye when he looked at me for too long a time.

＊

When they were gone and the sun had set, me and Jimmy had ice cream on the screen porch and listened to blackbirds settling down for the night like dark rain in the sweetgums out back of the house, neither of us talking right away but thinking hard on this development in our lives.

Well I guess he's all right, Jimmy said.

Well I guess he's not.

What did you think a that belt buckle a his? What do you call those blue stones?

They're turquoise.

I had a second helping of ice cream. I'd grown four inches since eighth grade. Coach Marr put me at outside hitter on the varsity when Tangie McCullers sprained her ankle so bad. Ice cream never gave me zits and I needed to maintain my weight with volleyball not half over yet.

You don't think she's all that serious about him do you, Chase?

Oh come on Jimmy. You know that look.

Yeah like you get when Casey Shields comes around.

I swatted the back of his head. Don't you smart off at me. We're just good friends.

Uh-huh. Do you think Claire Condra's a virgin?

None a my business and she's too old for you.

You a virgin?

And I plan to go on bein one. I swear to Jesus, that all you got on your mind?

Can you help me with my math homework tonight? They loadin it on already. Wisht I wasn't all that smart sometimes.

No you don't. Smart's the best thing you can be. Except good-looking, where you got no chance.

Jimmy grinned and punched my arm. He knew he was good-looking. He had Daddy's eyes.

Then he wanted to do something he hadn't wanted to do since he was maybe six, or during those weeks after Daddy died. Hold my hand. I guess I wanted to hold his hand too. Because I had this sense of dread, kind of like foretelling. I imagined Crow Tillman in our house of an evening, stretched out in Daddy's favorite chair with his boots off and a newspaper, or watching football on TV. And I kept seeing that buglight-yellow eye of his with the bolt of lightning grooved in it.

You know I'm always going to look out for you, I said to Jimmy. Because I thought he needed to hear it again.

Maybe, I thought, Aunt Tilly James and me could gang up on Mama—what did they call it when they snatched a soul from one of those religious cults? Deprogram her. Because in my estimation she definitely was that far gone over Tillman.

Claudelle Emrick was probably the most even-tempered human being I ever met. So good-hearted. Shamed to say Jimmy and me took advantage of her sometimes.

We were nowhere near Crow Tillman's league, as it turned out, when it came to taking advantage of people.

But, even like the most docile and sweet-natured hound it was possible to rile Mama. She didn't have a bad side and grudges were foreign to her nature. She did have a stubborn streak, and when it came out then it was time just to button up and leave her alone.

I didn't know what to do.

I got Jimmy started with his pre-algebra. He caught on right away. They had him fast-tracked in every subject. Like me. I wished Daddy could have seen the grades we were bringing home.

Daddy was an engineer who worked for the Highway Department. They double the fines for speeding in work areas along the roads but there's always some asshole. Daddy was in a coma for three days, then he died. Never opened his eyes. Not a word of good-bye.

Casey came by in his Jeep Wrangler, limping a little after football practice. We went for a walk anyway around our place and I kissed him a lot. I'd been planning to stay a virgin until I was eighteen but now there was Case so I was pretty sure I wasn't going to make it that long.

I told him everything that was bothering me about Crow Tillman.

Casey's second-oldest brother was a Jubilation County sheriff's dep and I hinted to Case that it would be a big favor to me if Von could find out about Crow. Who had said when I prodded him that most of his people were from down around Bainbridge.

Properties, I said to Casey. Yeah I'll bet.

Casey had a look around. The hoot owls were starting up. There was a big Hallowe'en moon, two weeks early. The air was nippy. I had my arms around him inside his letter jacket.

How many acres yall got here? Casey asked me.

Twelve. Five on the lake.

Figure what?

Figure two hundred thousand easy, I said. That's right now. Five years from now who knows?

Casey whistled.

Well that's it then, reckon?

Maybe, I said, but Daddy wasn't dumb. He knew better than leave it all in Mama's hands. Look, you know Mama. Bank teller don't mean she has a head for business. And other ways she's never been the sharpest knife in the drawer, God bless her. So Daddy had the property divided up and all twelve acres put in trust, eight of them for me and Jimmy's college. Want to go in now and I'll make some hot chocolate?

Sure.

⚊

A week later Mama took a couple of days at the bank and sneaked off to Cherokee, North Carolina, where she married Crow Tillman at Harrah's Casino and Hotel. Probably the most thoughtless thing she could have done to us. Aunt Tilly James and Uncle Wren were just slack-jawed. It was Crow's doing, of course. The son of a bitch had her hypnotized.

Mama was all apologies when they got back from their wedding trip, promised to do it again for our benefit in church. Like that made it okay. Jimmy said to me he felt like she had spit on Daddy's grave. Spit was not the word I had in mind.

Jimmy climbed up in his old treehouse that overlooked the lake. I spent hours coaxing him down, Jimmy crying most of the time.

The whole thing gave me such a migraine I had to miss the match with Pickens County. Just laid there in the training room throwing up in a wastebasket. We lost.

Everything was just turned-turtle in my life. I got a B minus on a pre-calculus test. First time ever.

Crow had given Mama a half-carat diamond ring he said had been a treasured family heirloom. In his family more than a hundred fifty years. I'd've liked to got that ring appraised myself.

He'd won close to twenty-five hundred dollars playing blackjack at Harrah's. Feeling real good about that. He gave me and Jimmy each a hundred-dollar U.S. savings bond. For our future education, he said.

Crow also said he didn't intend to make a big thing out of being our stepdaddy. We were a family now (going on and on about that) and all he asked for pitching in to help support us was some respect. I treat people how they treat me, was the way he put it.

Well not exactly as I soon learned.

✗

I met Casey and Von at the Burger King after volleyball the week Crow moved in.

Von Shields said to me, Well he's got a sheet.

Kind of expected that, I said. I reached for Casey's hand to get ready for the worst. A goddamned jailbird sleeping with my mother in Mama and Daddy's old bed.

But what Von showed me first wasn't so bad. Crow had been in the military (before acquiring the glass eye I supposed) and had done some kind of shady dealing. They'd busted him

down two stripes but gave him an honorable discharge anyway. So much for his army career.

Then there was something to do with defrauding migrant
workers down there in South Georgia, but how do you find a
migrant worker to testify in court? Charges dismissed.

After that, bar fights, ADW dismissed, possession dismissed
(twice). Domestic violence three times, but neither Vernelle
Cotter, seventeen, or Lacey Ann Spokes, nineteen, had been
willing to take him to court. I didn't have much trouble pictur-
ing what those two must be like. I went to school with plenty
of them. They did go to the trouble to get divorced from
Crow.

I sat there looking this stuff over, keeping a tight grip on
Casey. Lost my appetite so he finished my cheeseburger for
me.

You could say he's done·some dancin around inside the legal
system most a his adult life, Von said. But you know, Chase,
sometimes they get it out a their system and settle down okay.

I shook my head. The dogs ain't eatin that, I said.

I never had felt so hopeless and depressed, not even after
Daddy was run over.

Von looked sympathetic. He was one of those big good-
looking ole boys who don't have much of an eye for women.
The one he'd picked out to marry was as odd as a backward
duck.

Anything goes down out your way don't you be slow to give
me a call, Von said.

Or me, Casey said.

As it turned out, once Crow went off the deep end Case was right there with me.

If only he hadn't been.

Adam
December. Last Year.
Ten Days to Christmas.

It had reached that point where I looked for her around the campus every day, and was disappointed if I didn't see her.

This was almost four weeks after I'd first noticed her. She was tall, blond, with a hang-loose body and the soft appeal of sunflowers: a welcome glow of warmth and energy about her with another dreary New Haven winter setting in earlier than usual. She seemed almost always in a hurry, carrying a couple of books more than she could easily manage, both arms full and a bulging backpack. Sleet or snow, she never wore a hat, only a skier's headband to keep the precip out of her eyes.

Brown eyes, I was sure, although I hadn't yet come within twenty feet of her. And I was sure she wasn't aware of me.

Nobody at Yale paid much attention to their security guys unless there was a burglary or we had to cite a student for something. She had the workaholic's expression, not grim exactly but very preoccupied, running late for this or that as she hurried along. I didn't think she lived in one of the Old Campus colleges.

School had been closed for Christmas break, but there were always stragglers around. I was on duty until eleven, sharing the watch with Sven Griffith, who had had a root canal and was miserable. He stayed indoors keeping an eye on the squad room monitors while I biked my OC beat. A wintry mix was coming down. One of those raw blustery nights. I'd been reprimanded twice for listening to my iPod while on duty out there. But there wasn't a hell of a lot else to do: use my eyes, get rid of loiterers outside Phelp's Gate, check IDs occasionally. Count squirrels that hung around the campus near Yale PD looking for handouts. Some of them were brazen and could be a nuisance.

I perked up when I saw her again, coming across the slushy campus from the Saybrook Gate, heading my way. Her head down into the wind.

It seemed like a good night to finally get acquainted.

When she was close enough to where I stood in the shelter of the Phelps archway, near the steps up to our stuffy rooms, I said, "They're saying could be the worst winter in a decade."

She barely glanced at me, not breaking stride. As if I had nearly derailed some serious train of thought.

I thought she looked cold. Should've had her head covered.

"How about some coffee? New week, new pot of coffee."

All I got was a quick shake of her head, which she lowered again as she walked past me toward College Street.

I shrugged. Married, or living with someone, I thought. I didn't think gay. I guess I wanted to keep my fantasy going a little longer. Maybe I'd get another chance.

There's always traffic on College, and there are times when it's jammed. I watched her as she waited for an opportunity to cross. The wind had changed and she put her back to it, face down against one shoulder as cars went by.

Then she saw an opening and started out into the street. It's a long block. And even in this kind of weather some drivers were in too much of a hurry.

Good ideas to impress women always come late to me. I could've joined her while she was waiting on the curb, then stopped traffic to help her across to the New Haven Green. Time enough to get her name, at least, and find out if she was available.

Then I saw her do something both unexpected and dangerous: she stopped dead in her tracks in the middle of College, lit up by the headlights of cars going in opposite directions. One swerved away from her, missing by a couple of feet. Horns. She turned almost full circle, head high now, her mouth open as if she had cried for help. I saw that her eyes were tightly shut.

I ran toward her. A bus was coming, westbound. She was in its path. The driver was already on his brake, and the bus was sliding, back end coming around. If I had slipped or faltered I wouldn't have got to her in time.

But the bus came to a stop nearly sideways across two wide lanes as I put an arm around her and guided her back to the sidewalk by Phelps. For some reason her eyes were still closed.

I sat her down out of harm's way and used my flashlight to get stalled traffic straightened out, keeping an eye on her. But she didn't move from where I'd left her. Her head was in her hands.

"You hurt?" I said when I got back to her.

She shook her head.

"You can open your eyes now."

"Can't. Not yet."

I had once dated a girl who went to Wake Forest. The one I'd pulled off the street also sounded deep-down Dixie.

"What's wrong?"

She reached for my gloved hand on her shoulder, hung on tightly.

"Please," she said. "Just keep talking to me. So he'll know I'm not alone."

I took a fast look around. Traffic was moving okay. There were some people on the sidewalk wondering, like I was, what was going on with her.

"Who are you talking about?" I said.

"Would you help me up? I feel stupid sitting here like this."

I helped her up. She was biting into her lower lip.

"Please keep talking. Who are you?"

"The cop you didn't want to have coffee with."

"Oh. Yeah." She was trembling. "Recognize your voice. What's your name? *Talk* to me."

"Name's Adam Cameron."

"I think I—would like that coffee now."

"Right this way," I said, gently turning her around on the sidewalk. "Mind telling me your name?"

"Doesn't matter. Did I break any law?"

"No. You just came within a couple of feet from going under a bus. There's probably something I could cite you for if I think about it, but hell it's Christmas. Almost Christmas. And your name does matter to me."

"Why?"

"Because I'm falling in love with you."

Her eyes opened then. Wide. We were almost the same height. Her gaze was in a dead heat with mine. She wiped sleet from eyelashes and flaxen brows. Blinked. She had one of those slow wide smiles that begin with a curl at the corners of her lips.

"I'm Anne," she said. "Are you nuts?"

In the squad room it took her several minutes to settle down. She was skittish, obscurely out of phase, mind and body not connecting. She asked to use the bathroom. I had time then and probable cause to look through her book bag (her personal stuff was in a fanny pack that went to the bathroom with her), but as I had already declared myself to be emotionally involved, I didn't.

When she returned she was calmer, clearer, direct. She'd brushed her thick lion-toned hair away from her high forehead. Her face was classically elegant; it belonged on gold medallions. She wore neither lipstick nor eyeliner. Now that she was inside I noted a nickel-sized, almost perfectly round birthmark on the left side of her neck an inch below the ear. Nothing that detracted from her beauty.

She had a wonderful voice: Southern, low-pitched, and the mildly canted eyes of a young sorceress. They were bronze-green, thinking eyes, coolly observant. My heartbeat confirmed that I was in love with her. But I think I had been since that first distant glimpse. It happens that way, if rarely. Before you know a thing about her, hear her speak, know what makes her heart sing or shudder. She's the one. And the task is to find a way to be worthy in her eyes.

First, though, I handed her coffee.

"I broke out the vintage stuff," I said. "Two-year-old Sanka."

She gave me a skeptical look.

"I'm famous for my wit around here," I said.

"No doubt," she said. She held the mug in two hands and sipped some of the coffee. She'd taken off her coat. I noticed the sweater she had on was threadbare at one elbow. She sat with her legs crossed at the ankles. Long legs in faded butterscotch corduroys. Timberlands on her feet. She watched me over the rim of the mug. Not just looking. There's a big difference.

"Mind telling me why you couldn't open your eyes out there?" I said.

She sighed. "Medical condition. It's known as Essential Blepharospasm, or EBS. I call it "The Spaz.""

"Oh, that," I said. "Runs in my family too."

She knew I didn't have a clue, and allowed herself a smile.

"Right," I said. "Never heard of it."

Sven Griffith was wandering in and out of the squad just to check her out. I made a get-lost gesture she probably didn't notice. She was more interested in the last doughnut in a box of Dunkin's that probably had been around all day. I reached for the box and held it out to her.

"Help yourself."

She wolfed the doughnut down. Obviously hungry. Her Timberlands were old and scuffed and there was a toggle missing from the duffel coat draped over the back of her chair.

"So this blessed spasm is what?" I said.

"Blepharospasm," she repeated, wiping crumbs from a corner of her mouth. "I never know when they're coming. They last for two or three minutes. If I'm lucky."

"Your eyelids close involuntarily, and you can't open them? I think I read something about that. Maybe it was in *The New York Times*. But isn't Botox used to—"

"I'm highly allergic to Botox." She shrugged. "So I'm stuck with my . . . affliction."

"Sorry," I said. Half a minute went by with neither of us saying anything. "Look, the dorms are closed and I guess you're not headed home for the holidays. If you could use a place to stay—"

Her expression soured a little, as if I'd disappointed her.

"I've got a place. *Officer*."

"Well, no harm in asking."

"I'm a grad student. Applied Math. Scholarship. Grant money." She cocked her right arm to show me the wearing-out elbow. "Cheap sweaters," she said, with a rueful smile.

I felt a little embarrassed. "Four square meals a week. Maybe."

She sat back in the swivel chair and smiled again. A sympathetic smile this time.

"Been there?"

"Done that," I said. "Got the hair shirt."

She caught on right away. "Divinity?" And found it hard to believe. Outside of the fact that I was wearing SWAT-style kit and carrying a gun, I didn't look the D-school type. Apple cheeks, no straggly facial hair. But she seemed genuinely interested in my lapsed career.

"Why did you leave?"

"Theological issues."

"Lose your faith?"

I took my time answering. None of her business, of course. And I didn't know where she was at spiritually. A good many Southerners were born-agains. But it hadn't been an idle or a cynical question. She was interested. Not only in what I had to say: I felt as if I had passed a small milestone in her regard for me.

"Faith is an act of the imagination," I said.

She nodded, accepting my interpretation. Which told me she probably hadn't had a Fundamentalist upbringing. And I hadn't turned into Satan before her eyes.

"I got interested in what's real. A valid concept of the soul. Near-death experiences."

She did look away when I said that, and tension came into her face.

Probably I should have just dropped the subject then and there. Although we'd first had contact at a moment of imminent danger, still, dying wasn't a very suitable subject of conversation with someone I'd known for all of twenty minutes. But I was curious about her reaction, the way she kneaded one hand with the other. Like a child in need of comfort. A lonely child.

"A buddy of mine at the Frohlinger Center has been doing some far-out research into near-death experiences," I said.

"Far-out research," she repeated, glancing up at me.

"With enough success to convince me that, among other things, there isn't a heaven or a hell. No eternal reward, no fiery lake waiting for the undeserving."

She nodded, but not as if she wanted to hear more, uncrossed her ankles, and reached for the coffee mug she had placed on the floor. She leaned forward in the squeaky old chair and put the mug on the edge of the desk.

"Well, I—" she said vaguely, pausing as if trying to find a

way out of the conversation, "—never was much of a church-goer after I—I got to be a certain age. Around fourteen."

I wouldn't shut up, as if I were pursuing something secret in her, no idea of what it might be.

"Sergei is convinced that the soul—for want of a more scientific term—goes somewhere else after physical death. A place that, with our limited knowledge, we can't conceive of. Don't have a name for. 'The Other Side.'"

She smiled slightly at that, but the smile became a wince. Abruptly she stood. She moved like an athlete, looking for her book bag. "I really need to be—promised to drop some lecture notes off at the Taft. Anyway, thanks for the coffee, um—"

"Adam," I said.

"Right, Adam."

I was closest to the book bag and popped out of my own chair to retrieve it for her.

"I apologize for bringing up a touchy subject." I stood there holding the bag—it was heavy, bulging; I needed two hands—just out of her reach. "Have you lost someone recently? A family member, close friend?"

She winced slightly, shoulders tightening as if I'd somehow threatened her. I didn't think she was going to say any more. But there is this about me: I'm a good listener. I like most people, and it shows. I invite confidences. Probably I would have made a good cop, if I was interested in police work as a career.

She gave her head a slight shake that still betrayed discomfort, even pain.

"I've already lost—everyone there is to lose," she said.

"I'm sorry." I let it go. But I'd found out why she might not have travel plans for the holidays.

That made two of us.

I handed off the book bag but it was an awkward exchange. I lost my grip and a fat spiral notebook fell from an unzipped compartment, loose pages scattering behind and under the desk.

I went down on hands and knees to gather up the pages, which were filled with elegant Euclidean planes and dense formulae in her neat hand that were as foreign to me as Sanskrit.

"So far," I said, just to be saying something, "Sergei and his team have only used primates in their experiments at Frohlinger. Lowering body temperatures, stopping hearts for up to twenty minutes. Inducing clinical death. But although the animals are in a vegatative state, occasionally some of them show heightened brain-wave activity. Widely separated "islands" of preserved neural function. That's what is so intriguing. At the very least it contradicts nullibiety, don't you think? Postulates another plane of existence."

I got up and handed the notebook and pages for her to replace where they belonged in sequence. She stared at me as if I had lost her somewhere. Probably at "nullibiety."

"So if that plane of existence is reachable by losing a few heartbeats under controlled conditions—" I smiled at her. "I volunteered to go and have a look around. As long as Sergei can guarantee me a round-trip ticket. That, and a book deal."

Just kidding around—mostly—but her jaw hardened. If

we'd been on marginally friendly terms before, I'd lost my advantage. She stuffed the notebook away, yanked angrily at the balky zipper.

"Sorry again," I said, baffled. "What's wrong?"

"Life everlasting is for souls who have earned it. Cheat your way into the Netherworld through some sort of 'dying' experiment, and believe me you'll regret it."

"Netherworld? What's—"

"Your friend at the Frohlinger is right about another plane of existence," she said. "Not so far from us. You can be there in the blink of an eye. It's a mathematical conjecture I'm well on my way to proving. And—I've been there myself."

She wrapped her scarf around her neck with quick angry hand movements, possibly disappointed in herself for having said so much. Looking at me, looking away. I didn't move. I knew how to say nothing while subliminally opening the floodgates for someone who was desperate to be heard. And, probably in her case, not thought to be eccentric or a fool.

While she was putting on her parka and struggling with a toggle, I took a step closer and helped her with it. Buttoning her up. Reassuring that angry, unsure child with my touch.

"I drowned when I was a kid," she said, looking blankly at the floor between us. "Paramedics were—quick to get to me, and although I'd been in the water for close to half an hour, they were able to pull me back."

I did another toggle for her. Just nudging a breast under all the bulky outerwear with the back of my hand.

"From the Netherworld?" I said quietly.

She leaned against my hand for a few moments until the sound of a car's horn in the street caused her to jerk slightly, move back from me. I let my hand drop.

"Even after they'd resuscitated me, it was nip and tuck for a while. I was in a coma three weeks. I mean touch and go. Whatever. Anyway—" She touched an eyelid, a sad gesture. "I had this—quaint affliction when I woke up."

"Did you remember what it had been like, in the Netherworld?"

"Like here," she said. "But with some not very pleasant differences. Because—"

She didn't finish, just slung her backpack and started for the door without another glance at me.

"I'm off at eleven, Anne," I said. "Let's go for pizza and beer, talk some more."

"No thanks. I mean—don't bother."

"Look, I meant what I said. I really am in love with you."

From the doorway she looked back at me. Shook her head emphatically.

"I can't see you again." Unexpectedly, she smiled. "Thanks for saving my life. If that's what happened."

"A little dicey out there."

"Sorry about the busted romance."

"I'll always cherish the half hour we've had together. Why don't you want to see me again, Anne?"

"I'm not good at maintaining relationships." She bared her teeth; not much of a smile. "So let's just say we've never met."

She gave the sticking door a kick to open it wider and went down three steps to the archway of Phelps Gate. Shaking her blond head in some sort of defiant mood.

"And my name isn't Anne!" I heard her say.

✣

"So how did you make out with her?" Sven Griffith said to me a couple of minutes later when he came in to find me with my feet on the desk staring vaguely at the assignments chalkboard on one wall.

"It's going very well," I said.

He shook snow off his hat and helped himself to coffee.

"Oh, yeah? She looked kind of pissed when I passed her heading up College."

"This time maybe she'll cross at the light," I said. "Anyway, we're on for pizza and beer later."

"Ask her if she's got a friend. The good-looking ones tend to flock together." He was tubby and had lost a lot of his hair at the age of twenty-eight; only a little tuft above his forehead like a misplaced soul patch. There was something about Sven that caused women to roll their eyes behind his back. "What's her name?"

"I don't know yet," I said. "Thanks for reminding me."

I put my feet down and turned to the computer on the desk. Grad student. Applied Math. If she wasn't also lying about that—

In thirty seconds I had her photo on the screen, student ID, full name and home place, and her address in New Haven.

I whistled a happy tune.

"Can't fool a boy in blue, Chase," I said to her unsmiling image.

Chase
Jubilation County, Georgia.
Ten Years Ago.

Wasn't even a month after he and Mama got married that Crow Tillman started to hit on me. Not that he hadn't been looking me over a certain way since day one almost.

That old dog of his had bit Jimmy on the leg just out of meanness. Jimmy didn't bother him at all. Didn't like Angelpie. The bite wasn't real serious but none of us, Mama included, wanted to be around him after that so Crow gave in and built a kennel and dog run fifty yards out back of the house.

I was running two miles every morning to keep up my stamina for volleyball, running in the dark with a Boy Scout flashlight clipped to my belt soon as I got out of bed at six. I didn't need much of a light because I stayed off the roads and (dark or not) I knew the trails through the loblollies on our property up to the lakeshore.

The leaves had all turned, yellow poplars and sourwood, and most of them had fallen although it wasn't all that cold yet, just enough for frost in the mornings. Georgia can be like that south of the Chattahoochee National Forest and the beginning of the Blue Ridge, Indian summer some years almost to Thanksgiving.

The sky was lightening up by the time I finished my run back at the house. The morning I'm talking about I noticed Crow's silver pickup parked there by the kennel with a door open but I didn't see him until I was almost there. Smelled him before I saw him actually because he had one foot out on the running board although the rest of him was leaned back inside on the seat.

That wasn't all he had out. He was taking a piss. I almost ran close enough to get pissed on before I made a quick detour. Too late to run anywhere else except around the front of that high quad cab.

I wouldn't have made anything of it. Pretend I hadn't seen a thing and just kept going. But his old dog was out of the kennel and in my way and growling.

I stopped and tried to figure out where to go with Crow still pissing behind me like he'd swallowed half a distillery.

And laughing like a fool.

What ye doin up this time a night Missy.

It's morning, I said. Probably half past six.

I knew then he'd been out all night. Doing what? No surprise. I had a heartache for Mama.

Call off that damn dog I said. He bites anyone else in this family I'm callin the sheriff.

Reckon ye could say please, Crow.

All right. Please put Angelpie up.

Gotta tend to his business same as I gotta tend to mine.

Well you did that sounds like.

Crow got down from the quad cab behind me. I didn't turn around.

Maybe I got more business first. All sweated up ain't ye?

There's this tone of voice you hear when grown men are in a gamey mood. When you start to hear it depends on when you get your boobs. I'd been hearing it for three years almost.

I just want to go on to the house and get ready for school, I said. But Angelpie was still blocking my path.

Crow coming closer. I wouldn't look around.

Maybe I got business with you, he said.

No you don't, I said. And you can just stay where you are 'til you put that thing away.

What makes ye think I didn't put it away.

Cause you didn't that's all.

Well then I'll just put it away. If you're the kind a little gal favors takin them out for yourself. Like ye do with that Casey boy.

I don't do no such thing and I'm not havin this conversation.

Aw just teasin ye. I don't mean nothin by it.

Then he came on to me a different way.

Want a take a look at my picture book?

I'd heard about his picture book. It was dirty photographs

he'd taken himself and hung on a pull-chain from the mirror post in the cab of his Silverado.

No thanks, and you're disgusting is all I got to say.

Yeah well. Ye'd be surprised how many young ladies like yourself that's got good breedin and social standin maybe, how they will pull down their panties when you tell 'em you just want a take a picture of it. Kind of like a hobby a mine?

No I wouldn't be surprised.

Then ye wouldn't be surprised neither how that gets em so hot to please ain't no tellin what else they'll do with it whilst I keep snappin away.

The dog I said. Get your goddamn dog out a my way.

Say ye ain't doin it with young Casey? Bet he's got ye plenty ready for it though.

Not havin that conversation neither.

You got some sass, ye know that?

But I heard him zip up his pants.

Now that I'd stopped running for a couple minutes I was beginning to shake. I didn't want Crow Tillman to see me shake and think I was worried about him. Because I wasn't. Not all that much.

Why don't I just holler for Mama to come out and we'll get your thing settled right now, Crow.

I swear I ain't never seen nobody take a joke worse'n you do.

He whistled to his shaggy dog. Angelpie walked past me bright-eyed in the light from my flash. Black lip curled back over some wicked teeth. He gave a jump high into the bed of

Crow's pickup, bounding ground to tailgate just as agile as a skinny ole fox.

Now I looked at Crow. Wished I hadn't. He'd pushed that eye patch high up on his forehead. Bad eye a bad moon rising.

What were you doin out all night anyway? I said. There was fresh red mud on the silver body of his truck as if he'd been traveling back roads.

What little ye know be plenty nuff he said. Sometimes I work nights. Claudelle ain't mindin.

Yeah what kind a work.

Might need a see a fella I can't always see in the daytime is all. Now reckon as how we don't have no business together ye might as well run on in the house, little girl.

You can kiss my country ass, I thought, and took off.

No business *yet* was how it sounded.

It started with what must've been a promise in his mind and I didn't know how to stop it because he was just fishing to see if there was a lure I'd take and having a good time for himself doing it.

But he didn't put his hands on me one time so how could I tell anything to Mama and expect her to believe me?

She already had her hands full with Crow as it was. Right off he started in about our property.

When it was finally made clear to him that no part of our acres could be sold, bartered, or used as collateral for cash loans it began to get unpleasant at our place. Instead of being lovey dovey with Mama like he'd been those first weeks, he stopped joking around so much. His humor got nasty and all of a sudden Mama couldn't do anything to suit him. Whether it was how she cooked his eggs in the morning or ironed his shirts or how she did for him in bed. Crow carried on in a critical way like I said no matter if it was in front of Jimmy or me. To Mama's everlasting embarrassment.

Once he really got cranking with his run-on smart mouth none of us were spared. I'd give it right back to him. Jimmy would just burn and grit his teeth because sometimes Crow would give him a good shoving around too and pretend it was only fun.

Mama plain didn't know how to deal with meanness in other people. Any one of her sisters or Daddy's kin would've put Crow in his place, with a fist or a frying pan if necessary.

Or a gun. There were times when I heard Mama crying out of sight, because she never would do it around us, that I wished I had a gun. Jimmy's disposition was as sweet as Mama's but Crow got to him so bad sometimes (just funnin with ye, what's the matter can't take a joke) I'd see a look in his eye while he cleaned Daddy's twenty-gauge over-and-under after he'd gone bird-shooting with his buddies. Just sitting on the edge of his bed holding that shotgun across his knees. Looking at the wall.

From his expression I could tell, give Jimmy a few years and there wouldn't be nobody dare mess with him. But he didn't have a few years. That was the other thing I saw, or guessed, and oh God how it scared me. Not Crow himself. It was that unknown thing he'd brought into our house with him that got bigger and darker with every passing day.

✎

Our house was factory built and on the snug side even though it had three bedrooms. Jimmy's and mine and next to me Mama's that was bigger but seemed not big enough for the two of them. There were nights when I had to take my pillow and electric blanket and go sleep on the living room sofa with cotton in my ears. But Crow didn't sleep that much and might be in the kitchen at three in the morning, coming or going. Or he'd turn on the TV where I was and start talking to me no matter how hard I pretended to be asleep. Mostly he'd talk about how bad everybody was treating him in his own house and this wasn't the marriage he'd bargained for and by God Mama had better start seeing things his way or else.

When he rambled that way I knew he was worried but not about us. Something was eating on him.

He'd go outside when he had a cell phone call, and he had plenty of those. Or he'd hole up in the bathroom with the shower running so none of us could hear what he was talking about. There were times he'd almost run out of the house, jump into his quad cab and be gone most of the day. Or night.

When he was there he was walking into my bedroom anytime he thought he might have a chance to catch me naked. The builders' junk lock on my door had got broken and I knew by who.

I bought a padlock at Wal-mart and put it on myself. Mama didn't say anything to me when she saw it. By then she was looking worn-down on account of all the demands Crow made on her in and out of bed. She had dark circles under her eyes. She was a pretty woman before he came along, I mean Mama just sparkled. Only thirty-five years old. That was the effect he was having on her.

❦

We went to Aunt Tilly James's for Christmas. Crow excepted. At another family gathering or maybe it was a wedding reception he'd had words with Uncle Wren. Politics. Uncle Wren is dignified and slow to take offense. Still you don't want to get under his skin. He flat out told Mama he wasn't having Crow in his house on the Lord's birthday.

Another humiliation for Mama. She just swallowed her pride and took it because by then even Mama realized she'd made a mistake marrying Crow Tillman.

But she couldn't bring herself to call it quits. Give up on a sacred vow. Maybe she thought if she just hung in there and prayed to the Lord Crow eventually would change.

What he did was he just got worse.

❦

It was Jimmy who told me Crow was doing meth.

Tabs, not crank. Jimmy had seen him swallowing tabs with

tallboys while he hung out with some other guys at the BP convenience store on Talking Rock Road. There was meth all over Jubilation County. Most of North Georgia for that matter. The sheriff had busted a few labs. But most of it according to Von Shields was coming up from Mexico. Three years ago you never saw a Mexican anywhere around here. Now there were a couple dozen kids at our school spoke more Spanish than English. Spanglish they called it. I didn't have anything against them but some guys (none of my friends) said they were just another kind of nigger. They kept to themselves pretty much.

Anyway if Crow was already addicted when he murdered Mama in cold blood and wrecked everybody else's life I couldn't say. It was easy enough to spot one of those poor souls who were heavy into meth, oxy, or crack. But there's others who mostly use speed (according to what we were told at assembly when reformed junkies who were working now for Jesus came to lecture us on the evils) and they are able to hide their addiction for the longest time.

I suspect that was Crow. Hiding almost everything from us, his rotten soul, until it was way too late to do anything about him.

Adam
December. Last Year.
Ten Days Before Christmas.

Chase Emrick was living in an old three-story brick and stone building with a courtyard a couple of blocks up Edgewood from Old Campus. Borderline neighborhood. If you were a woman you wouldn't want to venture another three blocks north on your own, day or night.

According to the mailbox wall in the foyer Chase lived alone. That was encouraging. The building was a hive of grad students of many nationalities, most of them teaching assistants. Some young marrieds with small children or babies, judging from the strollers that were chained to the long radiator in the foyer.

I didn't want to buzz Chase. My tactic, such as it was, involved complete surprise, plenty of beer, and a six-course takeout Thai meal.

Which was still hot. Fortunately I didn't have to wait long for another tenant to show up and let me into the building.

She gave me the look that loiterers, even those carrying sacks of exotic food, deserved. I comforted her with a look at my badge.

"Who's having a kegger?"

"Just an intimate dinner for two. Sorry."

"My luck," she said wistfully. "Who is she?"

"Chase Emrick."

"Oh. The genius." She gave me a more speculative look. "So *you're* the one."

"There've been others?"

"No. I don't think so. That girl has a very cold shoulder. I figured the hell, her special guy's stuck in the Middle East with the troops or on the space station. Well, you two have a blast."

Chase's apartment was on the top floor opposite the stairs. Eighty years ago, I guessed, the building had been a showplace. Remnants of architectural charm remained. Marble stairs, art deco bronze wall sconces, carved balustrades of time-darkened oak, high ceilings and a snow-packed skylight overhead.

I had both hands full, so I tap-danced on her door to announce myself.

And waited.

There was a peephole in the door. She hadn't responded to my carefree toe-tapping but after a couple of minutes I had the sensation of being watched. I held up the twelve-pack of Bud

Lites I'd lugged over there with the Thai feast and tried to look guileless.

Moments later she undid the chain and another lock and looked out at me again, through three inches of door space. She smiled, more at herself than at me.

"Right. You *are* a cop. I underestimated you. Curiosity satisfied?"

"I hope you like Thai food, Chase."

"Never tried it."

"A lot like Chinese."

"So—you're thinking because you walked all the way over here in the snow with noodles and beer, I'm going to let you in?"

"Well—yeah."

She looked at me with only a little more encouragement than she might've had for a stray mutt on her doorstep.

"Trudged," I said. "I trudged. It's almost half a mile and you wouldn't believe how deep the snow is getting. My feet are numb."

She suppressed a laugh that started in her gut, shook her head, smiled secretly at some basic character flaw she imagined that she had, and opened the door wider, stepping aside.

I walked in and handed her the twelve-pack.

"This doesn't mean I need or want a boyfriend," she said.

"Just pretend you're under arrest."

She laughed at that too.

✤

Chase had a roomy studio, obviously fashioned from a larger apartment: there was a big fireplace that no longer worked. Dust mice eyeless in the far corners of the deep hearth. Not that she was a poor or indifferent housekeeper. The counters in the small kitchenette were tidy, what dishes she had neatly arranged on glass-front shelves. There were dried flowers tied with ribbon in a small blue vase.

Her sleeping arrangement seemed to be a yellow futon in one corner with an unzipped sleeping bag as a comforter. A gooseneck lamp for reading in bed. Pile of books around it.

"Want me to serve?" I asked her.

She gave me a slight but indignant shove out of her way and I wandered back to the big room where she lived and worked.

"The genius," as the woman downstairs had referred to her, and in truth it was like the lair of a genius child. Numerous colorful geometric objects ranging from pyramids and polygons to geodesic spheres hung from the twelve-foot ceiling, trembling at footfalls. There were two big chalkboards filled with formulae I couldn't begin to interpret (I knew a hyperbolic sine when I saw one, but information to the effect that "having shown [14], the lemma is implied by the following 'alteration' of [13]" with an accompanying foot and half of scrawled equation wasn't my idea of light reading).

The screen saver on her laptop was a hypnotic trio of icosahedrons rotating through and around one another like rigid universes in a deep purple sky. They mimicked a truly spectacular mural above the fireplace, six square feet like a composite of blowups from *Sky and Telescope* magazine, a favorite of mine. I recognized the Black Eye Galaxy, resembling a nest for a cosmic bird of paradise.

A casual look at her bookcases told me she probably wasn't eating regularly because she spent far too much money on rare books by superstar mathematicians. I felt a little intimidated. A math whiz. I loved her more every time I looked at her and I could go on and on about the Gnostic texts in relation to the Tanakh, but after that what would we talk about? Chase obviously didn't read fiction. She owned three computers, two of them verging on obsolescence, but she didn't have a TV.

Or family that she cared about, apparently. At least there were no framed photographs in sight. No pictures of anyone or anything except for a calendar of cats. Maybe Brad Pitt was hanging around on a poster in her bathroom, bare-chested and with thumbs tucked inside the waistband of his low-slung designer jeans, index fingers pointing at his favorite weapon while he grinned boyishly at her.

There was, I noticed, a bulky scrapbook or photo album on the lowest shelf of one of the bookcases.

"Let's eat," she called to me, as I was about to pull out the keepsake book and thumb through it, certain that Chase intended for me to feel right at home.

I forgot to mention that she'd dressed down for the occasion she hadn't known anything about. Chase was barefoot and wearing old but clean Yale A.D. sweats. She had scissored up the baggy shirt, turning it into a sleeveless bare-midriff outfit. Real cute. And distracting, while we sat on counter stools facing each other as we ate. At times I had trouble swallowing.

Chase had docked her iPod and we had Diana Krall for company. The smokey-toned vocals, good food, and a couple of beers relaxed her considerably. She still didn't do much talking, but she smiled at all the inside campus stuff I told her about.

When I ran out of gossip I asked her if she'd been a math prodigy back home in Georgia.

"Prodigy? No. I always got good grades; school was never hard for me. Math probably came easier than anything else. But after I—I told you that I drowned?"

"Yes." I didn't press her for details. She wasn't ready.

"Once I—recovered, I was—there were—differences." She touched an eyelid. "The Blepharospasm. I've never learned to drive a car. That wouldn't be such a good thing, would it? I'm not blind, technically, twenty-twenty in each eye. But still I have to think, sort of plan ahead when I'm outside, as if I *were* blind. Because I never know when I'll take a hit from the Spaz."

"Like tonight."

She nodded. "Usually I'm more careful about crossing streets. I was just fed up with things—the whole damned crowd at Applied Math. I only wanted to get home and—you asked about the math skills. Okay. It was as if the—as if drowning then returning to this world rewired my brain. Or woke something up in here."

Chase tapped her forehead.

"In those areas of math that most interested me, where I had been good before, suddenly I was phenomenal. There just wasn't much that was beyond my grasp."

I opened another can of beer. She looked at it, raised her eyebrows slightly.

"Maybe half," she said cautiously. "Been a while since I've done any drinking." She belched demurely. "Oh, shit," she said, and shrugged, which exposed the undersides of her full breasts. No bra. Her cheeks got a little pinker.

"Think nothing of it," I said, referring to the belch.

"It was probably the spices."

I poured half of the can of Bud into her glass. "Or the bubbles."

"Yeah, the bubbles." She grinned broadly. I was in love with a lot of things about her, and the Huck Finn space between her front teeth was close to the top of my list.

To distract myself I indicated the chalkboards flanking her computer desk.

"Working on your thesis?"

She drained her glass in two long swallows. Her lips curled in an ironic smile.

"It's just a little something that will change the landscape of twenty-first-century geometry. Most of the logic sequences are in place. But my Ph.D. adviser, Wurzheimer—the jerk—says it's not mathematics, it's metaphysics. Because *he* can't follow me, you see. Roving points of intersection between three-D and higher-dimension manifolds. *Way* beyond his ken. So he finds gaps in exposition to criticize, my 'difficult and abstruse notation.' Okay, math is about step-by-step rigor, but it's also about *depth*. I've done work in Ricci-flow strategies that, when I publish—it'll upset Wurzheimer's, and everybody else's fucking little applecarts. Jerks." She frowned. "Oh, did I say 'fuck-ing'? Excuse, please. I really was brought up better than that."

"I know."

"How do you know?"

"Mind-letters. We've been sending each other mind-letters while we sat here eating."

"Oh."

"The jerks you're referring to, they're the Applied Math crowd?"

"Don't get me started."

"Okay."

"I'm probably gonna lose my scholarship. And I say the hell with it. Was that in one of the mind-letters I sent you?"

"No. Why?"

"At Applied Math I'm known as 'that Freakout.'"

"I could go over there and rough them up for you."

She looked back at me, eyes narrowing.

"Oh, tough guy," she said.

"Far from it. But nobody gets away with calling my girl a Freakout."

"I'm *not* your girl. I told you. No boyfriends. No relation-ships. Uh-uh."

"Don't get you started."

"That's right. Don't get me started."

"So what applecarts did you upset already?"

"Ah."

She didn't say anything else. Then she got down from her

stool as if she suddenly were in another world, a somnambulistic trance, whatever.

"Mind doing the dishes?" she said. "I hate doing dishes."

Chase walked over to one of her chalkboards and studied it, only her eyes moving. She picked up an eraser and went to work on a string of equations, not getting rid of all of them, just making changes like a painter doing touch-up on his canvas.

I did the dishes.

After that I approached Chase and stood to one side of her, not saying anything while she nibbled her lower lip and scrawled with a piece of chalk. This went on for another five minutes. Then she was still, regarding her work. She put the chalk down and looked at me.

"Sorry. In the zone. Seeing everything dead-red, as the ballplayers say."

She looked tired and a little feverish.

"So this is—?" I prompted, pointing at the chalkboard where she'd been working.

"First installment of my freakout thesis that's derailing my Ph.D."

"I'm not quite sure what you're proving, I mean about the Netherworld."

"That it not only exists, often but not necessarily in mirror symmetry, but always with constantly fluctuating points of access between manifolds—that world, this one—that I call 'flexons.'" She exhaled audibly a couple of times and smiled happily at her work. "Oh—this is so *elegant*. So fucking beautiful! No one around here appreciates just how original and beautiful it is."

"The bastards," I said.

"At the least it's worth a Fields. Even if I get bounced from Yale, I've still got plenty of time. Just a question of money, but isn't everything?" She turned away from me so as not to yawn in my face. "God, am I tired! What time is it, Adam?"

"About one-thirty."

"You'll be going, then."

"If you say so."

"Well, you certainly will have to go," she said, sounding not at all certain. "That is, if I'm reading your most recent mind-letter correctly."

"I'll bet the snow is up to my knees out there by now."

"You'll have to go," she repeated, "because—your mind-letters—you do speak your mind eloquently, by the way—"

"Eloquently. Good word."

"Have to go, because the truth is, I'm on the same page. There. I said it."

"I know you are, Chase. So we don't need to say any more."

"Good," she said quickly. "You're *not* going. Can't imagine why you brought it up in the first—"

"Chase, I'd like to know about the other guy in your life, I mean, how serious is it?"

"There is no other guy in my life."

"Then who did you see and try to avoid when you cut across College Street and nearly got turned into roadkill?"

She looked away from me, reached up to switch off the hanging lamp above her desk.

"Oh," she said vaguely. "No, I didn't see *him*. This time he didn't come."

"Come from where? Who is he? Some guy who's been stalking you?"

She turned back to me and placed two fingers against my lips.

"Shh. That's enough. Don't give me a reason to regret this."

Her expression was momentarily hectic with unguarded grief.

What had been done to her? And who had done it?

Without the overhead light the room was much darker. With darkness it felt colder in the apartment. Drafty. Chase had been holding her other hand curled half defensively at her breasts. Now she let both hands drop.

I watched her walk to the futon in the corner. I just waited.

Chase looked pensively back at me, a long look. She turned on the gooseneck lamp and tilted the turtle-back metal shade toward the wall.

Then quick as a blink she stripped her cut-down sweat top over her head, let it fall to the floor and gave her tousled hair a shake.

I watched dry-mouthed and didn't move. Can't say I didn't move a muscle. But it's not a voluntary muscle.

In the bounce light from the lamp Chase half glowing, half in shadow. She pulled down, then high-stepped out of the sweatpants. No underwear. Flash of a bare knee raised like a salute. The other knee. And she kicked the sweats aside. Standing half dark half light hand going to one luminous hip in a statuesque study. The planes of her face sensual geometry. Faint curved glow of a C-section scar years old.

"Adam, come."

I went to her.

We passed into each other cautious as strangers, unreal as phantoms.

Chase
Jubilation County, Georgia.
Ten Years Ago.

It was April before Mama finally got fed up enough to throw Crow Tillman out of our house.

First she had the good sense to ask Uncle Wren and his oldest, Joe Boyce, to come over and back her up once Crow showed his face after a two-day absence. Boyce had played left tackle at UGA till he blew out a knee his junior year. He stood six-six and weighed about three-twenty now. Drove a mixer truck for Gage Brothers Construction.

When Crow finally got there (I heard all this from Joe Boyce later because Mama had sent Jimmy and me off for the weekend to her half-sister Mozelle's in Atlanta to help Mozelle and Clifton celebrate their twentieth wedding anniversary), Crow didn't go nuts like I would've expected. Probably because he was outnumbered.

Well he kindly shitgrinned and kowtowed you know, not meanin none a it. Them ole boys, you watch your back is all.

Tryin a worm his way into Mama's good graces again?

Surely was. Claudelle, she just handed his crap right back to him.

Good for Mama, I said.

So Crow Tillman took his things and his old dog somewhere else, which we heard was a hunter's shanty he borrowed off one of his drinking buddies. Left with a word of caution from Uncle Wren: Don't be a comin back when you think we ain't lookin for you no more. Uncle Wren, as I said before, was no big talker. But you knew when he meant business.

I never thought Crow had a yellow streak. Still didn't. But like Boyce said, he was one of those knew how to bide their time. And that worried me.

Was he talkin big when he headed on out? I asked Boyce.

Hardly didn't say nothin atall. Or he would have been in a right smart a pain.

Still I know he's plannin something. That's his style, Joe Boyce.

Don't ye be worryin none about him, Chase. Tillman can't set foot in Jubilation County again 'out us knowin.

I was still curious.

Whatall did Mama say to him?

Said the one thing she never could condone in other folks was dishonesty.

Well where Crow is concerned that could cover plenty territory.

Claudelle handled him just fine. Took too long gittinerdone in my estimation. But women can be slow to give up on a man, can't they?

~

I still wanted to know what finally made Mama do it. After three or four nights of talk about everything under the sun while we snacked and watched TV on her bed Mama finally told me, once she made me swear I'd never open my mouth about it to another soul.

What Crow had been pestering her to do was take out a loan (he called it) from the bank where she was head teller. Of course he had collateral for squat. He had an important business matter going he said. Needed thirty thousand cash. Mama couldn't take out a loan based on the equity in our house even if she was of a mind to do such a foolish thing because the mortgage was in all our names, not just hers. So what Crow was asking her to do was to embezzle (like it was just a matter of taking money out of a safe at North Georgia Federal Savings) thirty thousand dollars. Which he said he would give back in three days with plenty of profit left over.

It was a drug deal sure as hell. Couldn't have been anything else. Mama had to know that although she didn't want to say and really upset me.

Anyway she broke down and cried after telling me about Crow's scheme.

I thought it was a wonder he wasn't already doing twenty-to-life somewhere. Having Crow Tillman out of the house just had me feeling like I could breathe again.

Chase, I told him no over and over but he just kept on!

It's okay now Mama.

Then he said he'd already done his business deal and it was his life and maybe our lives too if he couldn't come up with the money.

Oh Jesus, I said. But Mama you know he's a lyin son of a bitch.

How could it ever come to this? How could I have been such a bad judge of character?

A smooth-talkin lyin son of a bitch. Oh Mama I know. You were just so lonely.

I did some crying too and we hugged each other until Mama had cried herself to sleep.

I didn't sleep, except for snatches the rest of the night. Hearing things that made me jump but otherwise I would never have paid attention to. Yes, Crow Tillman was a bull-shitter. But maybe, I thought. Just maybe there was some truth in him and we really were in danger from people we didn't even know.

God I hated him so bad.

Late April and Casey drove me home from school after dark. We'd been putting the yearbook to bed, meaning get it ready for the printer's. I was Freshman Features Editor. It was Friday night and Jimmy was playing baseball at Rehobeth Baptist Church. He was a catcher on their Little League team. Went to church there too because of Lurline Stott who he had a crush on. I went to church just often enough so as not to be thought a heathen but since Daddy died it really wasn't for me. I know Mama understood.

Anyway I thought Case and me would have the house to ourselves for an hour or so before Mama got back from her part-time job at the new Outlet Mall down 400 in Dawson County or else Jimmy's game finished up and he came home first.

I was expecting just a porch light on and maybe a lamp in the front room. But the house was all lit up. Mama wasn't home early because I didn't see her car. Didn't think it was Jimmy either.

Our house was in from the road about a hundred twenty yards at the end of an unpaved drive through pine woods. It was sloppy going after a good rain but for two weeks it had been dry. There was red dust over everything.

Not a car or truck in sight, but I had the bad feeling as soon as I stepped down from Casey's Jeep that we had a visitor.

Then I heard Mama say in a weak voice, Chase don't go in there. Get away fast.

I went cold all over. Looking around. Not seeing her.

Mama! Mama, where are you?

There, Casey said. Oh Jesus Chase.

Because Mama was crawling, elbows and knees, out of

some undergrowth thirty feet from us. Off to one side of the drive where the headlights of the Jeep barely touched her.

But there was enough light to show blood on her face.

We both ran to her.

Don't touch me, Mama said. Run. He's still in the house. Thinks there's money hid.

Crow Tillman?

Yes.

Crow beat you up?

Told him there wasn't any money. Chase, I can't move anymore. He tore me up inside.

Get her in the truck, Case, I said.

But when he tried to lift Mama from the ground she screamed.

No no don't move me. Get help both a you.

This was before every kid had a cell phone. The nearest phone to us that wasn't in the house was the Shell convenience store down the road toward town.

I pushed Casey away from me.

Case, go call the sheriff!

I ain't leavin you.

Do what I say.

Blood was bubbling on Mama's lips and when I tried to get my arms around her she screamed again.

Casey, go!

He ran to his Jeep and climbed in.

That's when the dirt-crusty Silverado truck of Crow Tillman's came from out back of the house and headed straight for us with swamp lights blazing. It was right on track to smash head-on into Casey's Jeep. Casey had to do a fast backup turn. Off the ruts of our drive he dropped into a four-foot ditch. He still had plenty of traction but he lost three or four seconds swinging around to face the highway.

With us all lit up like a carnival lot and the Silverado's radio blaring Waylon Jennings, Crow slewed his big quad cab to a stop in Casey's way. Casey had to hit the brake. There was no way for him to go except in reverse across the ditch.

That dog of Crow's jumped out of the bed of the pickup and went straight for Casey behind the wheel of his Jeep.

The Jeep was open, no door on the driver's side. Angelpie leaped up from the ground and grabbed Case's left arm.

Casey tried to fight off the dog and shift gears and drive at the same time. But Angelpie had his teeth locked in Case's arm and when the dog fell away from the Jeep Casey had to go with him.

Crow Tillman stepped down from his Silverado and took all this in. He was wearing denims and a rancher's straw tilted in a cocky way. I smelled one of the cheroots he was always smoking. His brand was Swisher Sweets.

Run, Mama said to me in a choked voice. She was swallowing her blood from something ruptured or broken inside. He's on some kind of dope, she said, and it's made him a crazy man.

I ran all right. Picked up a rock and ran straight at Crow. He never saw me coming. Five feet away I threw the rock, aiming for the back of his head. The rock weighed about three pounds and ought to have done some damage but all it did was knock his hat off.

When he looked around at me I was already scrambling backwards cursing my bad aim and intending to run into the woods. I knew he couldn't hope to catch me in his pointy-toed snakeskin boots.

The son of a bitch grinned at me. I saw he had a big black magnum Desert Eagle stuck inside his belt.

Hey, he said. Don't ye run off!

But I *was* running, for all I was worth.

I heard Crow whistle to his dog.

I knew Angelpie would come after me and wouldn't have any trouble catching up. So I just stopped.

At a girl, Crow said. He whistled again to call off his dog. Now come yere, Chase. You be the one a tell me where the money's hid.

You son of a bitch! Look what you did to Mama!

I started bawling.

Well now that's her own fault I got carried away, he said.

As if I was supposed to feel sorry for him.

We don't have money in the house!

I looked at Case. He was kneeling in the dirt holding his left arm. I could tell he'd been bit hard enough to crack a bone. His face was screwed up in pain. I tried to tell him with my eyes just to hold on and not attempt to make a break for it.

Ain't you the cunning little liar, Crow said. Like your Mama.

He started toward me. He wasn't all that steady on his feet.

I ain't havin none a it though, he said.

God damn you Crow Tillman!

It's way past time ye was learnt to talk to me with proper respect.

I looked at Mama lying there with pine needles stuck to the blood and dirt on her clothes and bare arms. She was whimpering but not wanting to move. I know it was because she hurt so bad. Proper respect? I was shaking.

Crow, she's fixin to die if we don't get her to the hospital! Look at her, Crow.

He wouldn't look. His face just got meaner.

Ain't botherin with that right now. Didn't hit her all that hard. She's just puttin on mostly. Now you and me's gonna rock'n roll, Chase, if ye don't change your tune 'bout that money.

I got some money in the house, I said. I'll show you where.

You mean that birthday money ye got saved? Done found it already but it don't mean shit.

I screamed at him.

Well that's the only money I know of!

Last chance a change your tune.

My mouth was so dry I couldn't say any more. I was shaking so bad my teeth chattered.

Okay, Crow said. Reckon ain't nobody a blame but y'ownself.

He turned, pulled his gun, and shot Casey through the heart. Knocked him over on his back. The gunshot was loud enough to be heard in the next county. Casey's face looked white and empty.

I must've jumped. I don't remember. I know I couldn't scream and if I did jump I was paralyzed right after. I couldn't draw breath. Still didn't believe what Crow had done. That Casey Shields was lying dead twenty feet away, his shirt soaking blood. We were going to have the house to ourselves for an hour. Now look. Everything started to get hazy.

Crow came over to me. Right when he grabbed me I projectile-vomited. He jumped back out of the way.

Well shit.

He pushed me to my knees.

Hung for a sheep, hung for a goat, Crow said.

The muzzle of that Desert Eagle was a couple inches from my temple. I could smell it in spite of some vomit that had come up in my nose. I was choking on vomit.

So they ain't no money.

All I could do to shake my head.

Just one a those days in't, he said. Giving my head a little push with the pistol like he was finding a place to put a bullet.

I started sucking wind.

Oh I ain't lettin ye go to waste, honey. Be suckin my cock too fore this night's done.

He turned the Desert Eagle around and shot Mama in the top of her head. Some of her blood and brains got on me.

I'd been to funerals and seen dead faces before. That's just how Crow Tillman looked after murdering Mama, except his good eye was wide open. But that eye might as well have been glass too.

Now get in my truck, he said. Got us some travelin to do.

I can't walk.

Didn't shit yourself did ye?

No I just can't walk!

Hell ye can't.

Crow took hold of me by one arm and yanked me off the ground.

Go get in the truck and be quick about it.

I was thinking about Jimmy. About what more could happen if he got dropped off from Little League right about then. With bodies already on the ground there'd be more shooting. Daddy, Mama, Casey, they were gone and I was a goner too sooner or later but Jimmy didn't have to be joining us.

I stumbled to the truck, my hands dangling and numb.

About the next thing I clearly remember we were in Crow's Silverado and headed north according to the signs I saw by the road. He drove with one hand holding the Desert Eagle in his lap and pointed at me. Should I have a notion of trying to jump out.

This was the first time I'd been in Crow's truck. Leather seats but still the cab smelled bad. All those Swisher Sweets and kind of a stale sour odor from the Appalachian Star quilt thrown over the back of the bucket seat I was in, riding with my feet tucked under me. Just a trace of Mama's favorite perfume in the patchwork of the quilt. I had the dry heaves. My eyelashes were sticky from crying. April 24 had been my birthday. This was the last day of April. I was barely fifteen. Crow Tillman was taking me somewhere isolated. He was going to fuck me all he wanted, then kill me and leave my body in the woods.

It's funny how after enough of it you just can't be scared any more.

Crow had been washing down speed with a tallboy while he drove. He pitched the can out the window and told me to get him a pint of Wild Turkey from the dash compartment in front of me. Said he had a big-time thirst.

There was a hunting knife in a scabbard Velcro'd to the top of the dashboard. Easy reach. I had a thought to go for it but my hand wasn't paying attention. Like it belonged to somebody else. Crow yawned and grinned at me. He laid that big Desert Eagle on the console between us. Cocked.

Go 'head, Chase. Give er a try. Knife or gun. Either one. Little ruckus gets my blood up.

I looked at him.

No.

No?

But there will be somebody to put you in hell for this.

Ain't no heaven, darlin. Nor no hell. No wrong nor right. It's all about what we can get out a this here life.

He winked at me.

Right now I got you, he said.

As it turned out I'd been right to be concerned about Jimmy. He got home only a few minutes after Crow left with me. Twenty minutes after that there was a statewide alert out with a description of Crow and Crow's Silverado.

Armed and dangerous. Hostage situation.

But Crow was taking some side roads and near forgotten bootlegger's tracks into the Chattahoochee National Forest to a campsite and picnic ground near the falls. The campground was deserted. There were a couple of cars at the overlook. I saw people walking in the moonlight. They were around a quarter of a mile away.

Holler and I'll cut your throat, Crow said.

He put me in the back of the quad cab and turned his dog loose to sniff around in the woods close by.

Then Crow did me. It hurt like hell. I never let on and I didn't say a word. Only good thing was he didn't last very long.

He told me to stay put then and got out of the truck. He walked in the direction of a big barbecue pit. Before he got there I saw him put the truck keys and the hunting knife on a picnic table.

There was still some fire in the barbecue pit as if somebody had had a picnic there earlier. A wire trash basket was stuffed with paper plates and cups.

I looked down toward the falls. Only one car was still there.

I didn't see anyone. Probably they were in the car. It was a makeout spot.

Crow was spending a lot of time by the barbecue pit trying to pee and complaining about it. He turned his head when he heard me get down from the quad cab.

Told ye to stay put.

I need to go too.

I didn't have to pee but I was bleeding because he'd been so rough.

I squatted though and looked around. The moon was almost full and the picnic area was as bright as twilight. The air was chilly, about forty degrees, and I was trembling. I didn't have much on.

If Crow's damned dog was around I didn't see him.

Crow still trying to pee, his back to me. It was hurting him.

Swear to God your Mama give me something!

That lie just seemed to wake me up. Filled me with such hate like I never knew before. Blaming my poor dead mother for something he'd got from a buckle bunny.

I looked again at the keys and knife on the picnic table. Then at the level ground between the table and me. Pine needles but no leaves. The ground looked trampled down hard.

It had rained steady most of the first two weeks of April. I knew the ground might still be slick. That old Georgia clay.

Man askin too much, you bitches keep your kitty boxes clean?

But he had his pecker running along with his mouth so I didn't have much more time.

I still had my shoes and socks on. My Doc Martens. I could run in them but not like they were Nikes.

First though I walked on eggshells the fifteen feet to the picnic table. Didn't want so much as to breathe because I was afraid he would hear me.

And I had to be careful picking up Crow's set of keys.

Next the hunting knife in my other hand. And I went for Crow.

I was almost on top of him, running flat-out, when I threw the keys in the fire pit and slashed across my body with the blade.

I'd aimed to cut him deep in the neck but as luck would have it the keys jingling past him caught his one good eye and he turned in time to get his right arm up. The blade sliced him below the shoulder.

Crow was loaded with meth and some oxy too but the combination hadn't slowed him down like it would a normal person. He was fast. He blocked me from sticking him in the armpit and with the hand that had been holding his pecker, he punched me in the side of the head. His rattlesnake hand Jimmy and me had been calling it.

I hit the ground rolling and without a knife.

Getting hit hard in the head didn't knock me out. It just made me slow and uncoordinated. Crow yelled something. I couldn't make out what. I had gone deaf in my left ear.

He came right after me, not breaking stride while he reached down to snatch the knife off the ground where I had dropped it. I could see I had bloodied him good, but that was all the satisfaction I was likely to get.

When I tried to get up I started to tip over. No balance. Crow grabbed me by the front of my unbuttoned blouse to keep me from falling down again.

I think he was mad enough to cut my throat then and there.

But as soon as he pulled me hard against him with the knife point under my chin he looked away in surprise, looked up at something that was behind me but treetop-high.

Then the picnic area was lit up like the football field at school on a game night. The loblollies green as emeralds and swaying in a local wind and tall shadows leaping every-where.

Crow's eye-patch face lit up too, pale as a death mask. He bared his teeth at the light and the source of the light in the sky. I was half deaf but I heard what it was.

Helicopters.

He dragged me to the truck, knife point still at my throat. I saw the helicopters over us like big old dragonflies. Someone was yelling down at us, a loudspeaker voice. Crow screamed back like a lunatic, sat me down on the running board of the Silver-ado and reached inside.

There was so much stuff blowing around I had to close my eyes.

He might have been fishing for an extra set of keys in the cab. But he couldn't find them. He had a chokehold on me. There were more lights flashing behind us now, the light bars on county and highway patrol cars. Six of them at least, a lot of law come for the kill, boxing in Crow's pickup.

That's when I guess it dawned on Crow, high as he was, he didn't have much going for him anymore.

But he still had me. And now he had his gun.

✗

Something came over Crow Tillman. It wasn't fear. By then hours into his spree I don't think he had the wits left to be afraid. What he had was a kind of maniac's excitement that pumped him, gave him extra strength. With me as a human shield and with that Desert Eagle in his rattlesnake hand I believe that in spite of the lawmen there he felt nobody could touch him. He was invulnerable.

Maybe in Crow's mind he'd become a movie star. The lights. The attention. The helicopters circling the clearing. All of the commotion had Crow ten times more excited and full of himself than he ever was while raping me.

Backing up most of the time, he walked or dragged me down to the footbridge crossing over the gorge below the falls. One spotlight or another never left us.

I guess he thought I was enjoying this as much as he was.

Reckon we're gone be on TV, Chase? Look up missy! You're with Crow Tillman!

You got to stop sometime Crow, I said.

Hell if I do.

Just stop now. Stop! Before they shoot both of us.

There were all kinds of guns pointed our way. High power scope rifles. They all stayed back probably thirty yards. Keeping a bead on Crow and me too because he held me so close it was like he was wearing me. Trying to negotiate with him through a damn bullhorn. That only ginned him up another notch.

She's fixin a be one hell of a party Chase!

Maybe if they all had just quieted down and stopped following us it could have gone better. The lawmen were ginned up themselves and likely almost as much a danger to me as Crow himself. From the way Crow was breathing I knew he'd wind down sooner than later. Even if he didn't know it yet.

But because of his chokehold I couldn't speak loud enough to put my two cents in. Otherwise somebody with good judgment might have listened to me.

Near the bridge Crow snapped a shot at a helicopter he thought was too close and almost deafened my other ear. By then I was looking for any chance to wriggle, bite, kick or gouge my way free of him. Wishful thinking. The muzzle of the Desert Eagle was against my head all the time, the bones of his wrist deep in the hollow of my throat. I was lucky just to be breathing.

Don't hear em shootin back do ye honey? Hell they's all scared to shoot!

The other side of the bridge there was nothing but bluff and thick woods. Maybe Crow thought he could lose the law in the woods. Helicopters and all. I didn't see any other reason for him to drag me across the bridge.

Below us the river was running swift beyond the falls. Even

in a dry season it was a tricky place to swim. There had been drownings. But it was some kind of a chance to get loose from him and not be shot.

Then we both got a surprise. Three guys in SWAT gear appeared out of the woods at the far end of the footbridge, throwing down on Crow with assault rifles.

Well looky here! Crow was grinning so big his gums showed.

And just like that he dumped me over the railing backward, caught me by an ankle before I could fall. I screamed, swaying in his grip sixty feet above the stony river.

I swear I saw Mama's face in the disc of the rotor blades of a helicopter hovering close by. And she was smiling down at me.

That's it Chase! Scream your lungs out! Tell em how Crow's gone drop ye down there if they don't back off and leave us be!

But I wouldn't scream for Crow Tillman. I dangled upside down in bloody underpants in the glare from helicopters. Calm inside because Mama was there and in a minute or two we'd be together again and happy ever after.

I won't scream, I said to Crow. *Because you don't scare me!*

I don't know what I expected from Crow. With the lights of helicopters filling the sky I couldn't read his expression. Maybe he smiled at me. I don't remember now.

Reckon we might meet up somewheres else Chase?

Oh shit, I thought.

What passed through my mind was, There could never have been a god anytime anywhere that would allow such a cruel and hurtful thing.

For all your sass, Crow said, I do admire ye, girl.

Oh shit.

He let out a Rebel yell.

Dyin don't get no better'n this!

Crow, don't!

I saw him do it. I saw him put the muzzle of the Desert Eagle to his head and blow half his brains away, a big red mist in the helicopter lights.

I saw it while falling from the bridge toward the river.

Adam
December. Last Year.
Ten Days to Christmas.

You know how it is if you're sleeping in a place you've never been before? The newness of it, the unfamiliar ambience and odors and what the film school guys call room tone seems to prey on your subconscious even when you're asleep. Little sounds: the rattle of a windowpane, cubes falling into the drawer of a refrigerator icemaker, steam hissing in old pipes, a voice in the depths of the building long past the witching hour: any of these is enough to jerk you awake, all senses alert and searching for a source. Especially that unexplainable sixth sense that can raise the hairs on the back of your neck for no good reason.

Chase lay on her side breathing through her mouth, a faint sibilance. She made a small sound of complaint when I disturbed the closeness between us. But my mouth was dry and

I wanted a drink of water. I got up from the futon as quietly as possible. It was cold enough in her studio for the air to bite naked skin. There was a night light in the kitchen and another in the bathroom behind a half-closed door. I found my under-shorts and sweater and put them on.

Three-thirty by my watch. I'd slept for only about an hour and a half but I felt wide awake. You have sex with someone you hardly know and usually it's just okay. Because bodies need time to get acquainted, a matter of comfort and trust more than lust. Sometimes it just doesn't go right at all. Social awkwardness more than physical incompetence. Both of you too anxious to please. I knew how long it had been for me. I didn't know Chase's sexual history. I knew at some point she'd had a child.

The faded C-section scar was barely perceptible to my fin-gertips, part of the chimerical mystery of her body. She tensed slightly when I brushed over the scar so I didn't touch it again. I went on to other things that relaxed and pleasured and opened her. Chase came quickly; for some reason I didn't. Knowing this, when I was out of her she lovingly grasped me with one hand. Wanting me to enjoy what she had enjoyed. Her eyes like bright water as she stroked me.

Now, I said, and she joined us again with a sigh of content-ment.

I told her that I loved her because it was true and because she needed to hear and believe that she never had to be alone again and I kissed her until her eyes closed and she slept.

At the kitchen sink I drank a glass of water, which seemed to go right through me.

In the bathroom I found that a window was open about an inch. Snow drifted in and glittered on the floor. I tried closing the window but it was stuck or frozen in the frame. I heard a sharp cracking sound and thought I'd broken the pebbled glass. Helpful Adam.

But when I looked it over I found that the window was undamaged.

I turned to leave and as I turned I saw movement out of the corner of my eye that gave me a quick deeper chill beneath my already cold skin.

The shock caused me to take a quick step back in the narrow bathroom and I burned my hip on the hot radiator. I needed a couple of seconds to recognize my own partial magnified image in a round makeup mirror attached to the wall on an extension arm between the door and the medicine cabinet above the washbowl. A mirror resembling a round opalescent eye that I hadn't noticed when I came in to use the john.

An eye with a brilliant deep flaw like forked lightning.

No way to tell how long Chase's mirror had been broken. But while I had tugged at the unmovable bathroom window there was no doubt I'd heard the sharp crack of snapped glass.

I am one of those who are superstitious about broken mirrors. If Chase was, or if she just couldn't see herself very well, she would have removed the mirror. So the break had happened spontaneously while I was in there. I had no explanation for that, but I felt a little creeped-out as I left the door slightly ajar behind me.

In my absence Chase had changed to a different sleeping

position on her left side, a hand curled thoughtfully beneath her chin as if she dreamed mathematically. Gleam of a single gold earring. In her sleep she possessed me. I filled my heart with the vision of her sleeping face but still there was a void. I needed more of Chase Emrick before I slept again. Not sexually. I wanted to see her life with her eyes, or the camera's eye, from infancy on.

There were baby and childhood pictures in the first album I chose from the low shelf of her bookcase, each meticulously identified in a woman's spidery handwriting on the back.

So I learned that Chase had a brother named Jimmy. Her mother's name was Claudelle and her daddy was Frank Chase Emrick Jr.

I already knew Chase was from North Georgia. Jubilation County. I saw her at age four riding a pony at a birthday party. Age five in cap and gown graduating from kindergarten. Age seven clinging to her daddy as they rode around Lake Lanier on a Jet Ski. At ten she had an armful of pet rabbit and a big grin that revealed missing front teeth.

The usual stuff, but all of it uniquely charming to my eyes.

There were a lot of relatives and occasions for reunions, all dutifully recorded with occasional sly comments (*Just can't get Addie to part with that dress it seems*). By Chase's mother I assumed.

The last photo midway through the album was of Chase and her middle school volleyball teammates. Nothing had been added since then. With the advent of the digital camera era and email photos the old family album had become a relic.

I heard Chase get up from the futon. She looked half asleep and foot-faulting as she crossed the bare floor to the bathroom, wrapped in a blanket Indian fashion. She glanced at me in passing, and at the album I had been browsing through.

"Hope you don't mind," I said. "Just getting up to speed on the Chase Emrick story."

"The story's not in there, and you don't know anything yet," she said. She went into the bathroom.

It was a quick visit. She still looked sleepy when she came out. Also she looked a little cross.

"My makeup mirror's broken."

"I heard it crack. But I couldn't tell you how it happened." My best guess was excessive heat buildup from the overachieving bathroom radiator and a draft of frigid air from outside.

"Not blaming you," she said. Still cross and with a frown niche between her amber eyebrows. She shuddered. "It's either too cold or too hot in here," she complained. "All the time. Last winter I had four colds."

She reached down and closed the photo album in front of me.

"They're all dead," she said with a forlorn pursing of her lips.

She walked to the bookcase and replaced the album.

"Your mother and father?"

"To begin with. And my brother Jimmy. My Uncle Wren and Aunt Tilly James who Jimmy and I lived with after Mama died. Casey Shields, my first real boyfriend. Dead too, suddenly and horribly. Maybe eight others. Related, not related.

Good friends. Anybody and everybody who has ever been close, special to me. They're all dead."

She turned to look at me with a bitter grin.

"Remember what I told you when I tried to blow you off? I'm not good at maintaining relationships."

"Doesn't make it your fault," I said. Not sure of what Chase was getting at. But she was shouldering a load of psychic blame and remorse, that was certain. She'd suffered from more than her share of unfathomable tragedy and at a young age. Enough to darken and warp anyone's perspective. Turn them against life.

Chase might have read some of my feelings in my expression. She looked away, shrugging uncomfortably.

"Did I just catch you analyzing me?"

"I hope not."

"I went to a psychiatrist for a while. He wore tweeds and cracked his knuckles. I thought he needed a shrink. They all do have their own analysts, as a matter of fact. Shrinks keeping an eye on each other. Is that creepy? Anyway, my guy had a word for what I was going through. *Psychalgia.* Extreme mental distress. Well, big discovery. He put me on tranks, of course, which more or less took my creative mind away from me. No thanks, doc. I'll manage to cope. And I did. And I do."

Then she looked at me again. "I'm not usually so talkative. Bet I've made you sorry you came."

"No."

"Have you seen a movie called *The Cooler*? It's about this dweeb who is so unlucky that a casino in Las Vegas employs him just to hang around the table where a gambler has a hot hand and cool his action." The grin was back, more bitter than before. "That's me. A different kind of cooler. But lethal. So long, been good to know ya."

"That's bullshit, Chase," I said with a smile to temper the anguish she was pushing deeper inside. "You haven't killed anyone."

"No, I just channel the one who does the killing."

After a few moments I said, "I think you must have had a nightmare."

"I don't have nightmares," she said. "Not in the usual sense."

Chase looked sharply at the cavelike fireplace nearby as if she might have heard Saint Nick dropping in a little early. She shuddered and moved away from it. The grin I hated was gone, her expression vacant.

"And I'm killing it now for you, aren't I? I mean, what was so good before." Her voice dropped to a whisper. "For us."

"No, you're not. You have something to say and it'll get said. Meantime . . . I saw hot chocolate mix on your shelf."

My suggestion broke the bad spell.

"Hot chocolate. Uh-huh. That's a good idea." She came into the kitchenette and busied herself. "Could I say something so dumb and clichéd you'll probably throw up?"

"I've always had a strong stomach."

"I've never met anyone like you, Adam."

"Good. It's settled. Tomorrow—no, this is Saturday already so probably we can't get a marriage license until Monday—how is Monday for you, Chase?"

"I do my laundry on Mondays."

"Yeah. Tuesday's probably better for me too."

"My daddy's not here to ask this question so I guess I better ask it. Do you make a good living, Adam?"

"Are you kidding? I'm a campus cop. My ends don't come anywhere near meeting my obligations. Forty thousand in student loans, and the interest clock never stops ticking."

"I'm broke too," she said, clasping her hands in a confessional way. "I did have a legacy but most of that money went for—"

She didn't want to finish the thought. She took a deep breath that ended in a tremor.

I put an arm around her and she just leaned, with eyes closed, until the chocolate was ready. She made it with milk. She also had Reddi-wip in the fridge.

"Secret vice," she said.

"Doesn't show on you."

"I can't get fat. You'll be happy to hear. I can spend half an hour doing nothing but staring at a chalkboard and I've burned like five thousand calories."

We sat down with our chocolate, turbans of whipped cream floating on top. Chase used her pinkie for stirring, then licked it and saw me smiling.

"Sorry. I've just always done that, since I was a little kid. Didn't matter how often I got yelled at. And I still can't break the habit. I get some looks when I'm in Starbucks."

"Not for licking your finger," I said. "Anyway I bite my nails."

"I talk in my sleep. I think I still do. Was I talking in my sleep?"

"No. A couple of times you were breathing heavily, as if you were finishing a 10K in your dreams."

"I have that dream a lot. But I can't run forward, it's always backward." She covered one of my hands with hers. "It was nice falling asleep with you, Adam. I haven't slept with a lot of men. Do you want to know how many?"

"Uh, well."

"Six, including you. Two of them were quickies, the same week. I recognized a pattern forming and put a stop to it."

"Were you married to any of the others?"

"No."

She sipped some of her chocolate, leaving a line of foam on her upper lip.

"I gave the baby up for adoption, Adam. No idea where he is now."

"I see."

"I was fifteen. So young. Still—I would have kept him. If the circumstances had been different."

"What were the circumstances?"

"I was raped."

I nodded, sad for her.

Chase put her cup down and looked for a long time into my eyes without blinking. Her next blink came with a tear.

"His name is Crow Tillman," she said.

At the moment she said his name there was no reason why I would have found it odd that she referred to Crow Tillman in the present tense, as if he still existed; because of course I knew nothing about him, his violent history.

⟋

If Chase had been on the verge of telling me more about what had happened to her, the onset of tears and the grief she had recalled changed her mind. She wiped away tears with the back of her hand. Then the look she gave me along with a tug of her other hand made it clear that she wanted nothing more than to go back to bed with me.

We made love again and took our time. Her last word to me was a soft and heartfelt "okay," and then she slept. Okay, I can rest. Okay, I don't need to be afraid of anything because you're with me.

I dozed but snapped awake after twenty minutes or so because of a subtle shift in my subconscious perception of the order of things in Chase's apartment, a disruption of the quietude that must have seemed ominous to me.

I lay still but fully awake and with a heightened pulse, straining to hear—what? An intermittent snuffling sound, along with a scratching of nails or claws on stone.

And what I heard was coming from inside the fireplace.

I sat up slowly. Beside me Chase twisted sharply in her sleep and moaned something, but she didn't open her eyes.

A furry brute of a dog walked out of the fireplace, stopped, looked around at me with greenish-yellow eyes. The dog appeared to be part chow and part something else and pure devil meanness.

I had been bitten by a neighbor's border collie when I was five and had no affection for even the smallest and most benign of breeds. I wasn't phobic and I had learned to deal with instinctive mistrust whenever a dog was near me. But the appearance of this animal with no warning caused my throat to swell nearly shut and my blood to congeal.

I looked quickly to see if the front door had been opened or had opened by chance in a cold draft, allowing the dog to come prowling into the apartment. But the door was closed and still chained.

I hadn't changed out of my uniform before coming to Chase's and my service pistol, a nine-millimeter Glock, was hanging on the closet doorknob seven feet away.

The dog made a low sound in its throat as it stared at me. A growl, but not the kind of ominous growl that signified attack mode. Only a warning, as if my focus on the nearness of my weapon was obvious to the animal.

You know when you're dreaming; even in an unfamiliar place you know when you're not.

The dog was very real to me.

Chase started in her sleep again as if she too felt its presence. But her eyes remained closed. So tightly closed I wondered if her eyelids once again were in spasm.

I had decided that if the dog made a move in my direction I was going for my gun, and good luck to both of us.

But all it did was show its teeth. Then it turned lazily away from Chase and me, turned around, and walked back into the fireplace. Its darkness blended with the sooty dark of the firebrick.

It walked in and simply disappeared.

Once my heart slowed I got up carefully, backed toward the closet while keeping my eyes on the fireplace, and slid the Glock out of its holster. Then I moved with the same caution toward the fireplace, or at least far enough to have a good angle of vision and some space between us should the dog be lurking there, waiting for me.

But there was no trace of it.

I started to shake then. Except for my accelerated heart rate, I had been almost nerveless before.

There was no dog. And clearly there was no way out of the fireplace other than up the chimney or across the stone hearth and into the apartment.

So what I'd seen so vividly could not have been real.

At Divinity school I'd had brief flirtations with combinations of drugs during my somatic crises and conflicts. Hoping that the mind-altering stuff would resolve questions of faith for me. Yes, I'd been that dumb, or merely desperate.

I hadn't dropped acid for nearly two years. But occasionally there were flashbacks, bad episodes that popped up during times of prolonged stress.

I wasn't stressed now. I felt happier than probably I had ever been.

Still I had to admit to the obvious. The "dog" had been an LSD sidekick episode. Over in seconds. I was fine now.

Except I shouldn't have been holding a cocked automatic when my hands were trembling so badly.

Chase seemed to have settled back into her previously untroubled sleep on the futon. But she had kicked off a blanket and after putting the Glock away I tucked it around her again.

There was no chance that I was going to go back to sleep.

I made coffee and borrowed Chase's computer that was hooked up to a DSL line.

Then I went exploring via Google the territory of Jubilation Country circa ten years ago.

To begin with I had only the name Crow Tillman. But his name yielded everything that Chase might have had difficulty telling me. The murder of her young boyfriend Casey Shields and her mother Claudelle. Her kidnapping. Tillman's self-inflicted fate and the fall into the river that nearly had killed Chase.

Old newspaper accounts and clips from Atlanta TV newscasts provided more names, useful cross-references. I learned of bizarre deaths that had plagued the family line after the death of Crow Tillman. Beginning with Aunt Tilly James, stung to death by a horde of yellow jackets in her backyard garden. Uncle Wren, shot in the back by a careless deer hunter.

Chase's brother Jimmy, at age thirteen struck by a piece of flying rock from a demolition site a third of a mile away. He had lived for nearly three more years, a blind quadriplegic, before dying of pneumonia. Another relative who had taken over the raising of Chase until she was of age had been killed by a train when her new car stalled at a crossing. A classmate who I inferred was Chase's best friend had been electrocuted in her bathroom during a freak electrical storm.

The medical bills for Jimmy Emrick must have been huge. Whatever the size of Chase's legacy, she undoubtedly had spent it all for her brother's care.

Information about what might have happened to the baby Chase had borne wasn't available. There was no birth certificate on file in Jubilation County. But she could have gone almost anywhere else to have him. Away from the gossip.

Although Chase more or less had told me that she'd been pregnant from the rape, I wondered if the father had actually been Casey Shields. Otherwise why carry the baby to term? Even though she hadn't had a strict religious upbringing, I didn't know how she felt about destroying a life, any life.

It became too sad for me to go on. I stopped looking into her past, preferring to dwell on what future I might have to offer Chase as I sat on a kitchenette stool and watched her sleep.

Then as dawn came I looked around her spare, businesslike apartment. A workshop more than a home. Christmas was nearly upon us, but there wasn't a tree, a wreath, a stocking hung by the chimney with care—nothing remotely appropriate to the season.

Chase slept on.

I got dressed and left her a message on one of the computers. Told her where I was going, when I expected to return, and left my cell phone number. I took a key from among those in a dish on the counter and locked Chase in.

＊

I walked the short distance from her place to mine, which was behind Payne Whitney gym and not far from the cemetery: three nondescript second-floor rooms. The fresh fall of snow had begun to dazzle as the sun rose. I whistled "Georgia On My Mind." Stopping a couple of times to make snowballs. Just feelin' like a kid again.

My roommate Saul was roughing it during the holidays on a bare-boat charter in the Caribbean. There were two messages from my mother on my answering machine, the most recent of which didn't disappoint me. Once again we would not be having Christmas dinner together in New York. That made four out of the last five.

"I know I promised we'd spend part of the holidays together, but unfortunately I won't be able to get away from Sydney before the twenty-eighth. But this will be the biggest commission of my career. There are matters to be settled. It's really a question of *my* artistic judgment. I suppose we shouldn't condemn politicians for not having good taste. Otherwise they wouldn't be in politics. Do try to call me on Christmas Day. Keep in mind there's a seventeen-hour difference or something like that. You know that I'm at the Intercontinental. I have a really nice view of Sydney Harbor."

When Mom ran out of things to say she just stopped and hung up.

"Terrific, Mom," I said to the empty apartment. I hadn't been to Australia or to many of the other places she'd also visited and graced with her work. But I wasn't envious. My mother and I had more or less gone our own ways since I was in prep but not because of disaffection. We tolerated each other very well while having nothing much in common. The art of child-rearing had been a great mystery to my mother. Almost as great a mystery as why I wouldn't take money from her no matter how tough things got for me. I liked myself better that way.

I showered, decided I was still a day away from my twice-weekly shave, and found enough clean clothes in my closet to be presentable. I had most of the day off; my shift didn't begin until four.

In my old Datsun I had a trenching tool that I used to dig the car out of a curbside pileup of snow. The Datsun started after its fashion, shuddering and coughing. I drove it over to the Super Wal-Mart off 91, checked my bank balance with my ATM card, and bought groceries, including a can of whipped cream. Ham, eggs, and bagels for breakfast.

In the tree lot I picked up a six-foot spruce to go with ornaments I'd bought, a star of Bethlehem that winked on and off. I chose a wreath for Chase's door. For the first time I could remember I was into Christmas in a big way.

So far the day was going so well I found a place to park on Howe only a couple of blocks from Chase's building. I lugged the tree and three shopping bags along slippery sidewalks to the foyer and rang Chase's bell.

She was up.

"Where've you been?" she said. "I missed you."

"Shopping," I said, over the intercom. "Surprises."

She buzzed me in.

I was overburdened going up the stairs. Both hands and arms full. The plastic sacks were tied off so I could hold all three with one hand, plus the bag of ornaments. I had hung the wreath around my neck like an evergreen target with a pinecone centered over my heart. The tree was just big enough so that, although it was bound with twine, I couldn't get a firm grip on the slippery boughs. I stopped a couple of times on the marble stairs, leaning the tree against the railing because my right arm was going numb.

The fat balusters were dark from age, carved with twining vines and leaves and bunches of grapes. The steep staircase, the stairwell, was not well lighted. Too many missing or low-wattage bulbs in the wall sconces. Management skimming by on maintenance.

Around the base of a baluster at the top of the stairs I thought I saw something move. But like I say the light wasn't great. And my eyes were still adjusting from the brightness outdoors.

Then I heard—and there could be no doubt of it—a rattlesnake's castanet warning somewhere above me.

In winter. In an apartment building in New Haven.

But rattlesnakes don't sound like anything else.

Another hallucination, I thought. Auditory this time.

I stayed where I was, listening. The sound wasn't repeated.

On the floor above me Chase unlocked her door and opened it a few inches. I saw her face.

"Adam, where are you? You coming?"

"Be right there."

I decided to shoulder the Christmas tree for the last leg up the staircase.

"A tree!" she said delightedly. "Let me give you a hand with that."

Chase opened the door wider. Light from the windows in her apartment brightened the upstairs hall and I saw the rattler coiled on the marble only a couple of feet from her doorway.

She started out and I yelled.

"No! Go back! Snake!"

I'm sure I heard it again, singing its ominous warning song.

Chase looked around in bewilderment.

"What?"

"Rattlesnake!"

She took a barefoot step out into the hall. "Adam, are you—"

The snake uncoiled but instead of striking her heel it slithered behind her and raced into her apartment.

"There it goes! Inside!"

I struggled up the last couple of steps.

"Be careful!" I warned again. The snake was full-grown, probably five feet in length. A monster.

Chase glanced at the floor past her threshold, looked back at me.

"But Adam, there's nothing—"

"I heard it and I saw it! There's a big rattlesnake in your apartment, Chase!"

From an expression of skepticism her face changed and became very very still. Her eyes, on me, lost their focus.

"Oh, shit," she said. "Not again, you bastard!"

Ignoring me, she turned and walked back inside.

"Wait there," she said. Then to my amazement she slammed and locked the door.

"*Chase?*"

She didn't answer me.

I called again, then put the sacks of groceries down, leaned the tree against the wall, and went through my pockets in a panic searching for the key to her apartment. At first I couldn't find it. I took some deep breaths, pleaded with her again to open the door. Imagining—but it hadn't been my imagination, or another residual LSD freakout. I knew what I had seen. And Chase was in danger.

I couldn't remember if I had left the key in a pocket of my Yale PD uniform. I was sweating coldly. When I forced myself to calm down and think, to visualize, I saw myself slipping the key into my wallet along with my spare Datsun key.

I had the right to carry a gun off-duty, a small revolver in an ankle holster, but today I had left it. Of all days.

I unlocked and opened the door carefully.

"Chase! Are you all right?"

There were no deadly snakes in plain sight. I opened the door wider, looked behind it. Nothing. But a shock went though me when I saw Chase. I closed the door behind me.

⚡

She was kneeling on the bare floor a few feet in front of the slightly raised hearth. Her arms were crossed over her breasts and her back was to me. She appeared to be staring straight into the unusable fireplace, a cave of antiquity, staring at one of the strangest objects I had ever seen.

It was three-dimensional, an elongate geometric figure sharply pointed at its vertices, with many shimmering surfaces, too many to count: they were silver and pale orange and vivid star-flecked rose. Or they had the iridescence of super-hot gas flames. The figure apparently was suspended in air, mimicking the less elaborate hexacontagons and icosahedrons that hung from Chase's ceiling and now were buoyant as party balloons, agitated by a strong draft above my head.

The figure was alive, no other way to describe it: as if it had taken form in one of the spectacular galaxies represented in the broad mural above the fireplace, drifted down from eons of Andromeda. The figure moved with physical properties similar to those of ball lightning, but much more slowly as it approached Chase, then drifted back toward the darkness of the fireplace when she raised a hand to it.

Her eyes were open, the pupils fixed. She seemed mesmerized. So was I. I had goose bumps. I had momentarily forgotten about the rattlesnake until Chase spoke to the object as if it not only had a strange form of life but also intelligence.

Or spoke to something far beyond it that only she could see.

"Snakes? I *hate* snakes! And I hate you!"

I touched Chase's shoulder but she didn't flinch or otherwise acknowledge me.

"So stupid of you, Crow! Because you've never scared me. You know there's only one way to the Netherworld. But I won't be going there again. It won't happen. You can't make it happen!"

Then Chase was silent for a long time, but not inactive. It seemed to me that she was attempting through force of will to push the geometric figure deep into the fireplace. Meeting with a lot of resistance, as if psychodynamically she couldn't get a grip on it.

"I don't want to hear any more of your shit!" she cried in exasperation. She sounded nearly out of breath from contending with a strange universe, a hostile god. "And I will never again let you get to me through someone else! You've taken enough from me. You will never take Adam!"

That startled and chilled me. I looked searchingly at the floating figure, hoping for a glimpse of whatever Chase was seeing. There did seem to be something at the figure's center point: amorphous, but a face. It wasn't possible to resolve that face. I made a brain-blurring effort, but it was as if I were trying to look into a hundred mirrors at once, the angles and planes constantly shifting. A fiery, brilliant kaleidoscope of combinations only a math genius like Chase could freeze into an equation, a precise rationale for an unknown dimension.

Then I heard something. We both did. The sound was in the apartment with us. A thin wail of a lost child.

Chase looked up, then at me. She started to cry.

"No! It can't be!"

I'd had enough. I brushed past her as she was getting to her feet and threw myself head-on at, and into, the figure above the hearth. Hearing Chase cry out behind me.

"Adam, no! He'll use you!"

But her voice had faded before she got the last word out. Her apartment, Chase herself, were gone.

And so was I.

It was as if I had taken a hard shot playing football, or simply run myself into an invisible wall.

I must have been out for a few seconds. When I came to I was on hands and knees with my head down. Feeling slightly nauseated.

I could hear nothing but the sounds of the internal workings of my body. Heart beating. My shuddering efforts to breathe. There was no external sound.

But there was light. A soft shadowless twilight gray.

I had to be kneeling on something that supported my

hundred ninety pounds. But I couldn't make out what it was. No texture of grass, gravel, concrete. A solid nothingness, which made no sense.

When I lifted my head—slowly, expecting pain, but there was none—something flickered in the twilight, a glowing spark that swept toward me then down and out of my field of vision, appearing and vanishing in only an instant, the tick of a watch.

Then there was another, from a different direction. Traveling with eyeblink speed, but definitely moving. Each brilliant and fascinating in its brevity and velocity.

Before long I was in the midst of a swarm of pinpoint streaking objects in colors ranging from deep orange to fiery red. Appearing, disappearing, but never touching me in their random flights. The source appeared to be a pencil-dot opening in the grayness and an unguessable distance away.

Still I heard no sound except for the rush of blood in my ears as I got to my feet.

The black speck from which the sparks emanated was enlarging on my still undefined horizon. It had become like an eclipsed full moon, with a ring of light around it.

I began to walk that way.

I found that walking when you have no dimensional reference and no sense of what is underfoot made for a daunting task at keeping my balance.

Adam! Can you hear me? I know where you are. But don't go any farther!

Chase's voice, sounding very faint.

Why not? I thought. Something was in front of me, and reachable. I felt no sense of danger. The sparks continued to fly and swarm, a universe of them through which I walked with growing confidence. Knowing how a god must feel. Charmed, powerful, creative. Galaxies at my fingertips.

No! Come back!

I tried to look around, still not understanding where I was but hoping to catch a glimpse of Chase. But just the act of turning my head upset my equilibrium again. I had to freeze in place to avoid a clumsy fall.

When I looked again for that defining full moon in feature-less space I was jarred to see a man somewhere ahead and on a plane with me. He was tall, with long black hair and an eye patch. He wore cowboy jeans and boots. He was grinning at me.

And like me, he cast no shadow in this place. But from the easy way he stood and tipped his hat in welcome, he seemed completely at home.

I stopped, making sure of my balance. I couldn't tell how far away he was. But there was no satisfactory way to reckon ei-ther time or distance here.

After a little while of looking at each other he gestured with the hat. Still with a friendly grin. Come on, what are you wait-ing for?

I heard him speak. But in that crushingly silent place his voice, his words, were all inside my head.

Give ye credit, ye done good gettin this far. Ain't no pussy man air ye? Like some a them others she has took up with.

Where am I?

Ain't nowheres jest yet. But keep a comin and ye will soon find out.

I don't think so, I said, suddenly wary. Taking a breath to find that my lungs were tight. I was no longer feeling confident and godlike. Who are you? I said.

But I must have known.

He waved his hat again.

Say ye don't recognize me?

No.

Well. We do have us a friend in common, if that be a he'p to ye.

Are you talking about Chase?

Little missy. All growed up now. But I knowed her first. In the flesh it were.

Rape is what it was.

She wa'n't mindin it so much. So ye do reckon who I am.

You're Crow Tillman.

I said his name with dread and loathing. My heart was beating as if I'd run a mile in snowshoes. Otherwise naked, because I was also bone-cold.

You are ready for the rest a us, mister honey. This way, if ye please.

No thanks.

Reckon I will just fetch ye on over then.

I moved, or tried to move, away from him. I wanted out of this place, but it was like being on the inside of an intact eggshell. I pushed against a membraneous, translucent whiteness.

When I looked again to where I thought Crow Tillman had been standing there was no sign of him. That eclipsed moon was back, probably twice the size it had been before.

Then from within the black circle of moon a dog leaped boldly as if it were part of a circus act. The same dog with a bear's rough pelt, a reddish chow ruff, and yellow eyes that I'd wakened to see prowling out of Chase's fireplace.

It came in bounding strides straight for me.

Before I could react to the threat I felt something pulling at me from behind, unbalancing me. I had the sensation of flying very fast and backward out of control, slammed one way, slammed another against invisible unyielding walls until I blacked out from the G-force of my withdrawal.

✣

The next thing I felt was being slapped, hard, in the face. My eyes smarted from tears.

"Cut it out!" I yelled.

I dimly made out Chase kneeling in front of me.

"Adam, you fool, you damned fool!" she yelled back, and smacked me a second time.

I tried to grab her wrist as she drew her hand back again. My fingers might have been boiled spaghetti for all the strength I had.

"What's the matter with you?" I said. "I think you cracked a tooth."

Chase sat back on her heels, sniffing. She was completely nude, crying and mad.

"How could you do a dumb thing like that? I almost couldn't break you loose from it!"

"The thing in the fireplace?"

"Yes!"

"You've seen it before?"

"Yes! I've seen it before!"

"What is it?"

"You wouldn't understand if I drew you a picture!"

"Can we stop yelling at each other?" I said.

For maybe half a minute neither of us said anything. I touched my jaw. Chase spat on her hand and rubbed gently where she'd hit me. She sniffed several times but the tears had dried up.

"I was in the fourth dimension, wasn't I?" I said.

"There is no one fourth dimension, Adam. They're all around us. Different shapes and sizes. Planes in space, some bundled with S points. Some with vibrational frequencies the human eye can glimpse now and then. Fraction of a second, too quick to assimilate."

"Chase, I saw Crow Tillman. It had to be him."

"Oh, hell," she said bitterly. "*Hell.*"

"It wasn't like any hell I've read about. So I must have been in the Netherworld, or close to it."

"You have no goddamn idea how lucky you are that I was able to get you out in time."

"Yeah, how did you manage that?"

"I just had to make it happen, that's all. You know about my condition. The Blepharospasm. Occasionally when I'm blinded it's as if my brain—hard to explain this. My brain gets souped-up. Thoughts are acts, according to Paracelsus. I saw you within a fourth dimension, a solid of rotation, although you wouldn't have felt any motion. You were like a fly on the wall of a doughnut shape called a *torus*. With the Netherworld tucked inside. I mentally grabbed hold. Otherwise you would've been stuck there, poor little fly. Lost forever, dear Adam."

Chase took a deep convulsive breath and came into my arms.

And that's where we made love, in one of the old reliable Kama Sutra positions, on her discarded robe in front of the fireplace and for the third time (counting back several hours). It was fast, explosive sex, no nuances. But even when we were too weary to do it anymore we still couldn't seem to get enough of each other. Carrying on. Sweet necking and peckings.

"What do you remember about the Netherworld?" I asked her.

"Oh—keep in mind that I only passed though it. Once I had drowned, wedged between a couple of rocks in the river and held down by the pressure of the water. That part of the Netherworld I visited was almost like home. I believe the Netherworld is different for different souls. Depends on how you come to be there, I think. For some it's a place of study and contemplation. Souls who plan to return to the earthly plane. The souls I met were kind. They were responsible for guiding me back to this life. Because I had more to learn here about myself. But where Crow is souls are in turmoil because they left our world too suddenly. Most of them committed suicide or otherwise suffered great trauma in passing over. They're angry and confused. Only a few are pure evil. They simply won't leave the living alone."

"Like Crow Tillman."

"As bad as they come."

"But he's dead."

"Suicides exist in a half-life state. They have a lot to answer for. If they're prepared to ask the right questions of themselves. Others just waste energy trying to get back here. A few do come through by means of a handy 'flexon,'—manifold wormhole—if there's someone on this side who—what's the word?—*enables* them."

"You're not an enabler. You must hate him with a fury that's hard for me to imagine."

"He comes against my will when my eyelids lock down. Another consequence of the—the Spaz that has me half-crazy at times."

"What does he do to you? Hasn't he done enough already?"

"He can't touch me, Adam. Or do physical harm to me. The others I've loved or cared about—they were fair game to Crow."

"How do we get rid of him? Once and for all?"

"I wish I knew."

Chase, still astride me, looked at me in that unwinking way of hers for a long time. Then she stirred and got to her feet.

"Need a bath," she said. "Now it really is time for you to leave me, Adam. And never look back."

"I was going to make us breakfast."

Chase shook her head.

"And never is a cruel word for a lover to use."

"But I mean it," she said.

"Think you're protecting me? I can handle myself okay. And if Crow Tillman isn't quite dead enough yet, let me deal with that."

"You have no concept of what he's like or what he can do to you."

I got up from the floor and we stood nearly eye to eye.

"He can't touch you or hurt you?" She nodded. "Then he's *my* problem. Crow and that dog of his. I've seen them. And I'm not afraid."

Chase said in her softest sweet-Georgia voice, "My last serious affair was two and a half years ago. His name was Jack. We'd talked about marriage. He was driving home late one night to visit his folks in Pennsylvania. The Beemer veered off the road and into the back of a parked eighteen-wheeler in the breakdown lane and Jack was beheaded. Witnesses said he wasn't driving erratically or too fast. There was no alcohol in his blood. His car wasn't found to be defective. It was just Crow. Again."

"I don't see how—"

"Adam. Listen. For eighteen months I was in and out of

clinics for treatment of depression. Crow almost got his way that time. He had me at the point of wanting to kill myself, even though I was very much aware of the consequences."

"Oh, Jesus, Chase. I'm so sorry."

"I'm better now. But I can't go through it again. Crow knows about you and he's crazy jealous so it's only a matter of how and where. Unless you're willing to be kind to me, and save us both. Please, Adam. Walk away now."

"I can help you," I said, although I had no idea how. Kindness? Obsessive love isn't kind, it's a mortgage on the flesh and soul. That was the state I was in. I wasn't thinking. I was desperate to hold on to her.

Chase shook her head mournfully and left me. Halfway to the bathroom she paused and ran a hand over the low back of a counter stool, not looking at me.

"Don't make me do this the hard way. If you're not dressed and gone when I come out of the bathroom I'll throw this through a window and start screaming and keep it up until the cops come. I'm already on the books as a freakout. But do *you* need it?"

"No," I said.

She drew a deep slow breath of resolve, stood tall, still wouldn't look at me.

"I *will* ruin your life to save it, Adam. Believe me."

I believed her. I also believed that she wasn't a wack job, because if she was then so was I. But if where I'd been and what I'd seen was only around some deep bend of reality then I could handle that because reality, as I knew from my existential cop-out phase with psilocybin and LSD, wasn't merely in the eye of the beholder. Chase knew it too, from a different angle of vision or perception. But I was certain she wouldn't be able to handle it much longer, alone.

For now she wanted some space. I didn't blame her.

"I'm going," I said, and began picking my clothes up off the floor.

She showed only a moment's anxiety (I was grateful for that, at least), by making a fist and clasping it with the other hand. She may have nodded but I wasn't looking directly at her. Then she went into the bathroom and closed the door.

"But I'll be back," I said.

Not for Chase to hear me. Only a pledge to myself.

When I had dressed I retrieved the groceries and Christmas ornaments and brought them inside. The shower was running. I leaned the Christmas tree against the wall beside the door. Then I scribbled my cell phone number on a pad and left it on the counter. I went out and locked Chase's door behind me.

I kept the key.

I didn't know how much time I should give her. I worked that evening, Saturday, then had a few days off. Chase's house phone was for her DSL line and I had neglected to get her cell number. There was a number in her file, but she had changed carriers recently. And there are no directories for cell phone users.

When I got off at eleven I drove to Chase's building. Her

windows were dark. I double-parked and looked at them for a while. Probably she was asleep. I wanted to be up there with her. I sat for half an hour shivering because the heater in the Datsun was erratic. I decided to let her sleep. Tomorrow had to be a better day. I'd come around and we'd have coffee at Starbucks. Talk through the morning.

I wanted to see her face with morning light coming through the window behind her. I wanted to see her smile at me.

At my place I lay awake until three a.m. staring at the ceiling. Thinking about Chase. Chase. Chase. A knot in my stomach, a fever on the brain.

I was back at Chase's building early and rang the bell.

And kept ringing.

She didn't answer.

On Monday, imagining all kinds of things, half sick from worrying about her, I got into Chase's building, went upstairs and used the key to her door.

The key didn't fit. She'd had the lock changed.

On Thursday I packed granola bars and a thermos of coffee and found a place to park not far from Chase's building on Edgewood, where I had a good view of the entrance. I watched for most of the day for Chase to come or go.

A poet named Richard Wilbur who I admired once wrote: *All that we do/Is touched with ocean, yet we remain/On the shore of what we know.*

The lines seemed appropriate to my growing sense of desperation. The daylong chill I felt wasn't so much from the December weather but from the fear that I might not see her again.

Never to ride her like a tiger swimming in the sea. Never her wilder secrets know.

Around four in the afternoon the New Haven cops arrived. I suppose someone in the neighborhood had noticed me hanging around and had ratted me out.

I was off campus and there was no point in pulling my own ID. The Yale police are about as popular as measles with NHPD. We don't work very hard, make more money, and have a better deal all around than they do. My excuse for loitering in my car—girlfriend hadn't returned from a shopping trip to New York and I was locked out of our place—sounded lame even to me.

They ran me and because I wasn't a known sex offender they told me just to go somewhere else until I sorted out my love life.

On Thursday night, three days before Christmas, I got seriously shitfaced for the first time in more than a year. Cycles of frustration, apprehension, depression: the pressure-cooker just blew.

The occasion was the annual holiday party at the Frohlinger Institute for Medical Research. I had no connection with the place other than my good friend Dr. Sergei Olanovsky, who generously had invited me to come by and indulge.

The Frohlinger bash is always large and boisterous, and by nine o'clock I wasn't the only drunk there. It's just that the others seemed to be having a hell of a lot more fun than I was as I leaned on the gallery railing two floors above the atrium and watched. There was a hot band and much abrupt, shrieking laughter.

"Merry Christmas." A woman's voice behind me.

"Bingle jels," I said, not looking up. She didn't go away.

"Looks like you could use a freshener," she said, referring to the empty plastic cup in my hand. "What're you drinking?"

This time I did look. She was a willowy black girl, more like chocolate-bunny brown, with flame-tipped bangs and hazel eyes, an air of casual bonhomie and a very nice smile. She also was wearing a set of velvet reindeer antlers with little bells that jingled when she moved her head.

"Scotch rocks," I said.

"Me too. Here, take mine. Haven't touched it. Fact is I've just been carrying it around—you know, one lone soul without a drink in her hand, the party just crashes. But I can't drink tonight, I'm on call."

When I hesitated, she extended the cup to me.

"Go 'head, take it. I'm pretty sure already you're not the designated driver."

"Thanks," I said. I tried to balance my empty cup on the railing. It fell off.

She saw my hand shaking but all she said was, "You bite your nails."

"Only in my sleep," I said. "But that's what straitjackets are for. Why do women always notice a man's fingernails?" I was thinking of Chase. I could be with a very pretty woman and Chase just kept forcing her way into my mind. Damn her, anyway; couldn't she understand that this was my night to drink myself into oblivion?

"Force of habit," my new friend said. "I have two kids who always need reminding."

"Oh, two kids." I noticed her left-hand diamond then. So she wasn't trying to pick me up. As if I was worth a second glance, the condition I was already in, with oblivion still a ways to go.

"Haven't seen you around the Institute before," she said.

"I'm new."

"I'm Linda, by the way. What's your specialty, Doctor?"

"I spesh, uh, lize in free-loading at other people's Christmas parties," I said. It didn't seem worthwhile to correct the mistaken identity.

"Looks as if you're very successful at it." Her smile negated any taint of sarcasm.

I lounged awkwardly against the railing, trying to think of something witty to say. Back at ya, kid. What I said was, "What do you do here?"

I saw Santa Claus with his big pack of goodies coming along

the gallery toward us. He appeared to be about seven feet tall and in spite of the Cloud Nine beard he seemed oddly menacing. I felt as if I were a kid again waiting in line at Macy's to see Santa, trying not to wet my pants.

"Resuscitation research," I heard Linda say. "Dr. Sergei Olanovsky's staff."

"Microwave any monkeys lately?"

She jerked her head back as if I had lobbed a spitball.

"Whoa! What have you heard about us?"

I gestured to correct myself. "No. No, excuse me. I'm a little drunk. You don't microwave 'em, you freeze the helpless little bastards."

Santa stopped abruptly in his shiny black boots, peered at me, then dropped his bag and lifted me off my feet in a bear-hug. I'm six-one and that's hard to do. Santa made it seem easy.

"Ho-ho-ho!"

I couldn't breathe but with my face a few inches from his I finally recognized who he really was.

"It's Dr. Strangelove," I gasped.

Sergei Olanovsky set me on my feet again. He needed very little padding to achieve Santa-like girth.

"Actually, my dear friend Adam, we treat all of our primates with utmost respect and care."

Linda nodded, eager to set me straight.

"The animals aren't frozen. What we do, we replace all of their blood with a cool saline solution that contains oxygen and glucose. When I say cool, I'm talking forty-five to fifty degrees. They go into cardiac arrest right away—"

I snapped my fingers. "Boom. They're dead."

"With no heartbeat, and"—she glanced at Sergei, who seemed to shake his head slightly—"usually no brain activity, they *are* clinically dead."

"But," Sergei said, "it is more to the point of our ultimate goal to say that they are in a state of suspended animation."

"For up to three hours," Linda said, beaming. She had real enthusiasm for their work. "Then we reverse the process, flush out the saline solution, rewarm them with their own blood, give their hearts a jolt, and—they're back."

"No harm done?" I said. "Sounds great. It's like I've been thinking—if there's intelligent design in the universe, shouldn't human beings and animals come with lifetime warranties?"

"Unfortunately," Sergei said, "there are mishaps. In a few cases, brain damage. So far, irreversible."

"I know this girl who told me she drowned when she was a kid. Thirty minutes submerged in some very cold water. She made it back. A few changes mentally and physically, but she's not exactly distressed goods. Anyway, the hell with her. Doesn't need me, doesn't need anybody. Monkeys are more fun. You can teach them sign language."

Sergei gave Linda a significant look, raising cottony stuck-on eyebrows. She smiled knowingly. I had outed myself as a love-lorn basket case. I felt a rush of self-loathing worse than the steady heartburn I'd been living with.

On the atrium floor rhythmic hand-clapping had begun, along with a chant of "SANTA SANTA SANTA!"

"HO HO HO!" Sergei serenaded them, then looked at me.

"So—any big breakthroughs, guys?" I said. "Any messages from the monkey afterlife?" I was feeling very smartass. Did I have something to tell Sergei about the afterlife!

"You forget, friend Adam, that we are a center of resuscitation research, with the goal of saving lives in trauma centers. Theological concerns—"

"Not on our radar," Linda concluded.

"But they should be," I said. "It's the one Big Idea that has obsessed the mind of man forever. *What's next?* we ask. But there's no need to look for a glimmer of brain activity in clinically dead chimps. Because it's *there*, Sergei. In the fourth dimension. One of them—they're all around us, fourth dimensions, I saw mat—mathematical proof of that. Didn't understand it. So what. I went there, I've seen it."

"Seen what?" Linda said.

Sergei looked at her as if asking, *How many has he had?* Linda shrugged. I felt a flush of animosity creeping up my neck.

"The *Netherworld*. I wasn't the only one. I mean, Chase was there too, ten years ago. She's the one I was telling—she drowned. She was clinically—forget about her. I'm trying to."

They were still calling for Santa below. The band was playing. The crowd was singing. *He knows when you've been naughty . . . he knows when you've been nice.* Bingle fucking jels.

"Time for me to pass out the goodies," Sergei said. He opened his spangled sack and began pulling out small brightly wrapped gifts that he lobbed to the cheering partygoers.

I was left with Linda's sympathetic eye on me.

"She busted you up pretty good, huh?"

"Don't know what you're talking about," I mumbled. I felt, childishly, neglected. Another bummer of a Christmas. I wanted Sergei's full attention. I had the most important news he would ever hear, the most important breakthrough of anyone's medical or theological career, and he was ignoring me by playing Santa. Holiday spirits and good cheer all around as he tossed presents. My mood went from befuddled to sulky and I wanted another drink. Then I had a brilliant notion.

"Time to quit monkeying around," I said to Linda. "Time to go for it." When she looked patiently bemused I returned to Sergei, tugging on Santa's sleeve. "I'm still top of your list, aren't I?"

Sergei/Santa looked at me over the straight edges of his costume spectacles.

"Now, Adam. We were merely speculating. Amusing ourselves. And perhaps a little too drunk on that occasion."

He returned to sailing beribboned packages out over the atrium.

"What's going on here?" Linda said with a humorous rolling of her beautiful eyes.

"No!" I protested to Sergei's red velvet back. "Listen. If it can be done, I'll do it. First astronaut to the Afterlife."

"*What* is he talking about?" Linda asked Sergei.

"Complete nonsense. Adam my old friend, maybe you should sit down for a while."

"No!" I shouted again. "You don't understand! Everything's

breaking up around me! I don't know what to *believe* anymore! I've seen things—" There was a metallic taste of fear in my throat. "But I have to go there again. Not to be afraid, and—and to bring back evidence. Understand? *Proof* of the most important discovery—nothing less than salvation for humanity! None of us ever need to be afraid anymore of what's to come as long as we fulfill our moral and speershel obligations here. Don't you realize? What that could mean to *you* personally? A fucking Nobel in medicine! I can make it happen for you, Sergei!"

Sergei had emptied his gift sack and, I dimly realized, was out of patience with me.

"Try to keep your voice down, Adam."

"Will you listen to me?"

"Now it is you who should listen. A Nobel in medicine sounds very fine. But we are not ready for human trials in our research. That will come, I am sure. With the cooperation of a trauma center that, perhaps, receives accident victims who will surely die if they have suffered cardiac arrest from loss of blood and must quickly be placed in pre-op suspended animation."

"Primates are one thing," Linda said. "But to induce arrest in an otherwise healthy person, then attempt to revive—so-o risky, and a legal black hole. Not just a career-breaker, it's—"

"American gulag," Sergei said, in a dismal un-Santa-like tone. I was furious with him.

"Where the *hell* is your scientific curiosity?"

Linda was being beeped. She checked her pager and looked at Sergei.

"Ten to one it's Honeychile's preemie. I'd better get over there." With a swift look of reappraisal she said to me, "Pleasure meeting you, Adam. Why not just send that nice girl of yours some flowers?" She walked briskly away from us, the bells on her antlers jingling.

"Always works for me," Sergei said.

I must have been glaring at him.

"How about some black coffee?" he said. "There's plenty of fun yet. A couple of women I could—"

"The hell with that," I said. "You're not interested in my proposal, fine. I got close to the Netherworld on my own, I can do it again." I thought I saw alarm in Sergei's lachrymose dark eyes. "I'll get the proof, and *I'll* get the Nobel. Thash one prize my mother hasn't collected yet."

"In the meantime perhaps you can get some rest. I see that you have not been sleeping well. Then—Friday we'll have lunch? I will listen very carefully to what you have to tell me. It all does sound—remarkable."

He seemed sincere, not coddling me. I knew I had been acting badly. He could have just blown me off. I nodded, feeling a flush of gratitude.

"Thanks, Sergei."

"I'll change now and drive you home."

✦

Sergei and I met for lunch on Friday at York Pizza, where he was partial to their lasagna. Two days before Christmas and with the school closed the restaurant wasn't crowded. We sat at a table in the back.

He listened to my story (and Chase's) politely but didn't offer much comment other than to express an interest in meeting Chase. I told him I wasn't giving up on her, that I didn't believe she'd really meant it when she told me I should get permanently lost.

Sergei shrugged, humoring me.

"Ah, the women," he said as we walked out of the restaurant. "The more elusive they are, or should I say pretend to be, the more it enhances their desirability."

"Can't get her off my mind. I brush my teeth, I see Chase in the mirror. I feel like I'm going crazy."

"Crazy, friend Adam? Lately I've come to believe that it is our obsessions that keep us sane."

"And produce the occasional lottery winner," I said. I was able to smile.

I stepped out into the narrow street to avoid a woman with three small dogs on leashes. And barely escaped being killed.

Construction work was in progress on the York Street side of Sterling Memorial Library and the sidewalk across York was boarded off. The weather had turned just mild enough to pour concrete. A ready-mix truck was backing up with its warning beeper going. Backing up slow, which didn't matter because I slipped on a patch of gutter ice and sprawled backward almost under the wheels.

If the driver had been looking in his side mirror he probably wouldn't have seen me—it happened that fast. But he had the cab window down and his head partway out and he caught a flash of my plaid parka as I went down. Maybe Sergei or the woman with the dogs screamed. I don't know. I know the truck stopped close enough to my head that I could smell axle grease.

I'm normally agile and it hadn't been much of a misstep. But just as my foot slipped I'd had the sensation of being solidly pushed into the middle of the street.

Sergei pulled me back up on the sidewalk. I was stunned and shaking. I looked back at the ready-mix truck.

"Does that make you a believer in Crow Tillman?" I said with a nervous laugh.

Sergei just shook his head slowly, not an act of denial, but a comment on the precariousness of life in general.

Looking up at the Gothic face of the library, I saw a third-floor window shining brightly, as if reflecting the sun. Only one window.

And the day was overcast.

The brightness faded after a few moments.

I hadn't eaten much for lunch, but what there was had turned to a lump of ice in my stomach.

✎

On Saturday morning I was patrolling on my bike around Old Campus when I saw Chase for the first time in more than a week.

I'd just passed the rusty sandstone mausoleum of Skull and

Bones, heading toward Chapel. She walked out of the Star-bucks across from the British Art Center wearing her familiar headband. After a gloomy Friday the sun had returned. Chapel's sidewalk was filled with last-minute shoppers.

Chase hesitated, put something in her coat pocket that could have been a Metro railroad timetable, and pulled on her gloves. I kept going past the Yale Art Gallery and called to her.

She looked my way with no show of recognition, not even a wave. She turned to cross York but the light had changed and there was traffic. I caught up to her on the bike.

It *was* a railroad timetable sticking out of her pocket. Amtrak's northeast corridor schedule.

"Going somewhere, Chase?" I said.

She didn't look at me. "I might be."

"Time to talk?"

"Don't do this," she said.

"I'm off at four."

"No."

Others waiting for the light were curious or amused. A deeper shade had crept into Chase's already-red cheeks. But except for that healthy glow it looked as if she hadn't been sleeping well either. Her eyes were tired.

"Chase?"

The light changed. She squared her shoulders but didn't move.

"It's Christmas, Chase. And I'm not working next week. We could—"

She glanced at me then. I saw tears.

"Just leave me alone!"

Then she was gone, nearly running across the street.

I was on shift, and couldn't follow her. But there was no need. I wasn't discouraged. I knew that however much I loved her, she also wanted and loved me, and her heart was breaking.

We were going to work this thing out, because we had to.

Jingle bells.

Christmas Day at noon I carried red roses to Chase's apartment.

The door was open. The apartment was cleaned out, except for four packing boxes in the center of the room designated for pickup by one of the storage places around town.

I let the roses drop on her threshold.

"That one's available first of the month," someone said.

I looked at a man with a collie on a leash who had let himself out of an apartment down the hall.

"Do you know who—"

"Name of Emrick." He noticed the roses. "But she's gone."

"I see that."

He followed his dog down the stairs.

"Merry Christmas, bud."

I walked inside, looked around. I don't know what I expected to find. I looked into the cold empty fireplace. Then I turned, picked up the roses I had dropped, and ran down the stairs, remembering the Amtrak timetable in Chase's coat pocket yesterday.

✎

The only picture I had of her was her student ID photo. Not the greatest likeness, but it would have to do.

After leaving my Datsun in the parking structure next to Union Station I went inside to find that there were a surprising number of travelers on Christmas Day. I paused on the gallery by the newspaper rack and looked over the lobby floor. I didn't see Chase.

Three ticket windows open. The second clerk I tried studied Chase's photo, looked at the badge in my other hand, and said, "Ayuh. She bought a one-way on the one-eighteen express."

I looked at my watch. It was fourteen minutes past one.

"Where was she going?"

He handed back the photo. "Philadelphia, believe it was. She a fugitive?"

"Dangerous to lonely hearts. Can I buy a ticket on the train?"

"Cheaper at the window. Philadelphia, now that'll cost you—"

I looked at the board above the stairs to the tunnel that led to the dozen tracks into the station. The one-eighteen Acela was on track two.

I ran like hell with a dozen roses in one hand.

The Acela had arrived and most of the passengers had boarded when I reached the platform. Once again I didn't see

Chase. I had cause to wonder how accurate the ticket agent's memory was. But the train was about to leave. I had to take a chance that Chase hadn't changed her mind and was already inside. I got aboard and ten seconds later we were leaving New Haven.

I had three bucks left in my wallet, plus my last pay check, after the conductor sold me a ticket. To New York.

Then I went looking for Chase.

✧

She was in the fourth car from the rear of the ten-car express, eating an apple and looking out the window. I paused in the aisle, just looking at her.

"I saw you get on," she said.

"What a coincidence this is."

"I think we stop in Stamford. I'm going to have you arrested for stalking me. They'll put you off the train."

"If I'm going to be arrested," I said, "I might as well deserve it."

I sat down beside her. She looked at the roses I was holding. I think she meant to smile but then her chin wrinkled and she bit her underlip.

"Damn you, Adam," she said in a weak voice. "It's just no good. When are you going to get the message?"

"Maybe when I'm sitting in the Stamford jail. But I doubt it."

I kissed her then. By the time I finished kissing her, Chase's face was wet and she had a grip on my shoulder like an eagle's claw.

Our faces were five inches apart. I saw the rest of my life in her swimming eyes, and was content.

"Oh, Adam. Adam."

"Why are you running away?"

"Wasn't time not to," Chase said with a forlorn grin.

"What about your graduate studies?"

"A case of quitting before I get fired. Limit the damage. Anyway, my work will be my reputation."

"I didn't have enough money to go to Philadelphia. I had just enough on me to get to the Big Apple."

"So this is good-bye? Again?"

She patted my cheek, regretfully I thought.

"What's in Philly that's so important?" I asked her.

"Nothing, really. Don't know a soul. It's always better that way."

"Don't you have any math buddies anywhere?"

"Like Newton, I've never been big on soliciting other people's opinions. Hanging with the Establishment in-groups. There are a couple of geometers at Advanced Studies down the line in Princeton. I know them by way of the Internet. They haven't been hostile to my conjecture. I was thinking of using them to vet my proof pre-pub. But that's two years away." Her expression was a little dreary. "Three years. Never."

"You could go to Philly tomorrow," I said. "Or next week. What's the hurry?"

"Well—"

"Here's an idea. I have a place to stay over in Brooklyn. A loft. Big but comfy."

"Oh. Who are you staying with?"

"You may be cutting-edge in circles and triangles, but you're a little slow in real life."

She was a big girl, but she snuggled just fine. And closed her eyes.

"Thanks for the roses." She sniffed. "They make my nose run, but they're beauties."

"Jingle bells. Could I have the rest of your apple? I didn't eat anything today."

"Oh, baby. Of *course* you can have my apple."

I took it from her and had a bite. I munched happily and watched suburban Connecticut rocket by outside.

"To think," I said, "it all started with an apple and a wily serpent."

Chase snuggled a little closer and sighed.

"Oh, baby," she said again. "You don't know the half of it."

Chase
December. Last Year.
Christmas Day to New Year's Eve.

When I came out of the bathroom Adam had fallen asleep on the big waterbed in the living quarters of the loft.

Looking down at his contented face, that wide brow smoothed now and Byronesque tumble of hair, I felt at least half in love with Adam while thinking glumly and superstitiously how we are often ruined by choices made, not in haste (although he'd overtaken me like a storm front) but by a desire to know innocence once more. So here I was, still glowing in the flesh, unprepared for new life, new times, hard times, the great risk of loving a man more innocent than I could hope to be again. Love hides all flaws and disasters, for a little while. I was reminded, to the point of tears, how deliciously we had clung to each other, consecrating our addiction. Trusting unspoken vows of recklessness.

Instead of lying down, I obeyed an instinct to prowl and know unfamiliar space, another woman's lair.

I covered Adam, then went exploring in my clogs and one of his mother's thick warm practical robes. The floor-through waterfront loft was spectacular, but with skylights and eighteen-foot ceilings and huge windows it had to be a bastard to heat.

The building, converted into artists' studios and apartments, had been a four-story brick brewery directly on the East River across from Lower Manhattan. The night river was eel-black at low tide, shining with the drowned lights of two cities. A low freighter coasted between bridges on its way to the sea. I looked at topless towers that were burnt gold in a winter haze and thought about nothing much for a while.

✒

"Your mother's a sculptor?" I had said to Adam when we stepped off the freight elevator directly into her studio.

"Yehp."

"Who is she? I don't know much about—"

"Stella Moritz," he said.

"Oh my god! Really? I know *that* name."

"She's famous." Then with a shrug and that wistfully comic face he puts on, "But to me she's just—*Mom*."

Adam turned on more lights.

"She has another workplace out on the island—a converted hangar at an abandoned navy airfield where she does her really big pieces. Stuff that has to be shipped overseas on the decks of freighters."

"This is so cool," I said, gawking around. There was a lot of welding equipment, chain hoists hanging from the ceiling, bins of scrap metal, works in progress—or some of the pieces that stood seven or eight feet high, many resembling ungainly exotic birds trying to take flight, might have been finished for all I knew. "Where is your mom?"

"Stuck in Sydney, she says. Although I wouldn't mind being Down Under this time of the year. It's summer there. But she could jump on a plane just any time now."

"So I'll get to meet her."

"Be brave," he said cryptically, and picked up my duffels. "Meantime we bunk in Mom's digs."

"Adam, you didn't bring any clothes with you."

"I keep a few things here for when I'm in town. But I plan to be stark naked for the next couple of hours. Make that the rest of the day. Day and a half?"

I gave him an elbow in the ribs and we went up a couple of steps into what looked like a stage set—as big and almost as open as the studio.

Bamboo screens and hanging tapestries divided the kitchen, entertainment, sleeping, and bath areas. But the only real privacy was afforded by what back home would have been a double outhouse on a rural farm. *Way* back in the hills.

"Mom has this whimsical sense of humor," Adam said.

"I love her already." I wasn't paying much attention to him. It was the antique bathtub on a granite slab beneath a skylight that had me gawking again. You could learn scuba diving in a tub like that. There were painted silk scrolls on a surrounding brass framework that could be let down around the tub for semi-privacy.

Chinese or Japanese scrolls. When I was closer I saw that the scrolls depicted certain acts. They were discreetly erotic. Not pornographic.

The rest of Stella Moritz's living quarters was a treasure house, filled with paintings and native sculptures she'd collected around the world.

Adam made a fire in a flask-shaped Oriental stove and took a bottle of wine from a teak rack.

And after the wine we got the hang of making love on a waterbed.

Before Adam fell asleep I said, "Is there a chance we could stay here like, forever?"

"It can get noisy at three A.M. when Mom's on a creative jag."

"I don't care."

He smiled and before drifting off kissed the spot on my neck I had told him was a birthmark. But it hadn't showed up until I was fifteen, either on the night my mother was murdered or while I lay in a coma afterward. I knew what it was: my mother's blood. It would always be there to remind me whenever I looked in a mirror that I had failed her, and Crow Tillman lived on in the Netherworld.

I hadn't forgotten my resolve to be on another train or a bus tomorrow to somewhere. Anywhere else. I had let my guard down, pushed it all aside for a little while. Along with the cold unhappy darkness of me.

Because, after loving him and lying with him and looking into his face, Adam reminded me so much of Casey Shields.

Reminded me of myself: or who I could have been, if Crow Tillman had never happened to me.

✗

The day after Christmas we went to Rockefeller Center to ice skate.

Adam was good at it. I'd never been on skates before, but I have the ability to pick up anything athletic quickly. No collisions, no pratfalls. In ten minutes I mastered my toe and sliding stops. Before we left I was skating figure-eights around him. I have this competitive streak too.

"Try a parallelogram," Adam said, pretending to sulk.

After skating we walked a few blocks to the Museum of Modern Art, where four of Stella Moritz's sculptures were in the permanent collection and another, a Solomon's seal composed of black marble and burnished steel, was on loan from a Rotterdam shipping magnate.

"Steel, granite, hand-hewn timber. Mom likes rough textures. That also seems to be the case with the men she takes up with."

My favorite at the museum was the mermaidlike figure made entirely from the rusted links of an old freighter's anchor chain.

"How long do you think it will be before she rusts completely away?" I said, feeling a sort of romantic melancholy as I looked up at her. The figure on its pedestal was nearly two stories high.

"We could stand here and time it," Adam said. "But I'm hungry."

On our way to dinner we stopped at a bookstore for coffee. Adam bought me a book with beautiful photos of almost everything his mother had created during a thirty-five-year career.

"Now you two will have something to talk about," he said. "Planes and surfaces and the genius of Stella Moritz."

From his slightly wry expression and tone I couldn't tell just what he thought about his mother. But anyone would have to be in awe of her talent.

The restaurant was a mirrored and candlelit cellar-dwelling place off Third where almost all of the staff seemed to know Adam.

Cozy and expensive. I couldn't believe the prices. After years of scrimping and often coming up short I had frequent anxiety attacks about money.

I whispered to him, "Adam, are you sure about this? You'll blow your whole paycheck."

"This is one of Mom's hangouts. She's treating us."

"You finally got through to her? When?"

"While you were taking a break at the museum she gave me a jingle from the Sydney airport."

"She's on her way home?"

"With a stop in Budapest." He shrugged. "That could be for a day or a week. I didn't ask."

"Are you intimidated by her, Adam? I mean, my God, I would be."

"Put it this way. She's always been more of a mythic mother figure than an actual mommy. Mountains are quarried for her to make statues that stand in front of palaces." He smiled. "She'll show up sooner or later. Meanwhile we're livin' large on Stell's tab. Every now and then I let myself do that."

"I hope this doesn't sound mendacious, but isn't she—?"

"Oh yeah, worth a few million," Adam said indifferently.

"But—you're paying off student loans?"

"I just like earning my own way. Painful as that gets sometimes. There are trust funds. First one kicks in when I'm thirty."

"Adam, I know something about your mother. You've never said a word about—"

"My father? Stephen Cameron. A painter. Died when I was thirteen. A riding accident. My mother never married him. She didn't marry any of her lovers."

"Married to her art."

"Sure. She's totally selfish, like most creative people I've met. But there's something pure about their selfishness, a childlike purity, if they're any good. If they're not any good then they're just a pain in the butt."

"So you're an only child."

"Mom tended to be a little careless about birth control. I have a half sister who's an investment banker in Hong Kong and another half sister who works in New York for one of those supermarket magazines that make big hoopla of the little sins of celebrities. But Dory's a pal. She'll route us to some of the best New Year's Eve parties in town."

I was smiling when everything went black.

"God damn it," I said, lowering my head instinctively and shielding closed eyes with one hand, hoping that no one at nearby tables was paying attention.

"You okay?"

"Yes. It's the spasm, the Spaz. I can high jump and throw a ball with either hand, but I can't keep my eyes open when I want to. Just talk to me. Did you have a relationship with your father?"

"I did. I miss him still."

"What was he like?"

"Well—his career never really happened, but he didn't lose his passion for art or life. He was a man who always seemed on the verge of being overwrought. A man of great emotion, hunger, ambition. Everything about him outsized, like his canvases. Gestures, embraces. He could maul you with his enthusiasms, his brio. I spent summers with him. The usual exchange program. He was about to marry a Frisco socialite when his horse threw him. Head-first into a tree."

"Do you have a picture of him?"

"Mom has a self-portrait in one closet or another at the loft.

Keeping it for me until I settle down somewhere. You're shaking, Chase."

"I'm sorry. There's never a guarantee—"

"That your eyes will open again?"

It wasn't what I'd been thinking about.

"Would surgery be a possibility?" he asked me.

"There's a chance I'd wind up with one or both eyelids permanently at half mast. No thanks. I'm too vain."

I felt his fingers on the back of my other hand, which was on the table. I felt another, contrary touch, cold, on the back of my neck.

The spasm lasted another half minute, and then I was looking at Adam again. Gratefully.

"You're still here," I said. Because a weak joke seemed better than saying nothing.

The maître d' had approached our alcove table with a solicitous expression, then his eyes darted to the small vase of hothouse amaryllis to one side of the starched linen tablecloth.

The amaryllis had not simply died; they were blackened.

The maître d' whisked the vase away.

Adam turned to look at the departing vase, looked back at me with a tense smile.

"Leftovers from a bad magic act?"

"You know what it was. Is. Life is a mystery and ultimately defeat. What life is not is a fantasy. No matter how weird it seems to get."

I suddenly felt drained, headachy. The headaches sometimes came on after an episode of EBS, and they could be fierce.

I rubbed my forehead, keeping my head down, not wanting to look at Adam just then.

"So how does he do that? Muck around with the bloom time of some cut flowers in a vase? What dimension is Crow Tillman inhabiting right now? Is there anything to keep him from walking in here, pulling up a chair, sitting down with us and ordering his escargots Bordelaise with a youthful but cheeky Muscadet?"

He was nervous. But, I thought, more angry than nervous. Trying to get a grip on an alternate reality.

"We've discussed this. He's sort of dead."

"Not all the way dead, just sort of. Earned his ticket to ride to the Netherworld by blowing out a chunk of his skull and half of his brains with a cowboy cannon."

"He's missing brains, but brains are a matter of matter. Matter, of course, being what we make of it perceptually."

"We're talking vibes here."

"We're talking alternate reality. The Netherworld."

"Which is not fantasyland."

"Strictly fourth dimensional, the one closest to our plane of existence, or vibrational level, that you blundered into like a gored bull."

"It wasn't my fault. If the Netherworld is able to interact with our own, then it's a bad design job. Who do we blame it on?"

"Oh, blame it on me, the rogue interface, the irrational-dimension-whatzit." I took a pinch of salt from a pewter service and dropped it on the tablecloth. "Speaking of design. Pick one of these beauties. Any single crystal."

He frowned as if he thought I was about to start telling fortunes.

"Fourth dimensions cling to one another like these grains of salt," I said. "One purpose might be to build bigger and better dimensions. I haven't worked all that out yet. It might take a lifetime, if I have a lifetime. For now it's enough to understand that although they are vibrationally beyond our five senses, there are uncountable dimensions surrounding us, passing through us. The Netherworld is here"—I separated a crystal of salt from the others with a fingernail—"or here"—I flicked another off the table, then raised my hands in a slow half circle above my head, fingertips not quite touching. "Or here, in the space between my hands. Get it?"

"No. But I like listening to you talk."

After a few moments I said, "Adam, it's one thing to put up with a semi-invalid with freaky eyelids who should have Boy Scouts helping her across the street, but—*this*. Devil. This—monster—who won't let go, that's too much for—"

"For you to handle alone. But we'll find a way to make him let go. Just stop running, Chase. I waste too much energy tracking you down. Which I am prepared to do until you spit in my eye and tell me how much you hate my making love to you."

We looked at each other and I enjoyed what the candlelight did to the motes in his eyes. The wine steward brought a bottle of something that was probably worth a month of his tips. I liked wine but to me it was just grapes and a shitload of fetish.

When we were alone again I said, "I faked all of my orgasms, Adam."

"Try selling that to one of your hypothetical Boy Scouts," he said.

It might have been the good wine, or something that was also very good in Adam Cameron's eyes that put a stop to my headache before it dug in for the night.

Once more I pushed all the other stuff back and just had a wonderful time. Got drunk slowly. Laughed a lot. Thinking, hoping.

Maybe.

Maybe this time it can be different.

✣

But Crow was jealous. And Crow has no patience.

✣

About those episodes of Spaz (as I call it): there's never a way to tell when one's coming, like a slap in the face from someone I never see. But without the pain of being slapped. It's hideous and unexpected but painless. Sudden darkness. After so many years of it I still cringe. Struggle for a few scared seconds to open my eyes, knowing it's hopeless. The release will come when it comes. It has taken up to ten minutes. I might go a week without having one, then it can happen three times in a day. Doesn't seem to matter if I'm sad, happy, bored, frustrated, or PMS. But when they snap down, a truck driver used to lifting seventy-pound crates off the tailgate couldn't pry my eyelids open one millimeter.

So there I am: temporarily blind and it can be an awkward situation. Or potentially dangerous. I've learned to be subconsciously aware of just where I am at all times, in a strange room or on the street. In case. Or else.

The human body is full of little quirks and oddities, practical jokes of the flesh I guess.

Uh-hum, Adam murmurs, his head against my side (he could use a haircut), ear against my breast. He has nice ears. Small, neat, like a faun's although I've never met a faun. I just know they're cute. He's half erect again after, what, twenty minutes? I haven't had a lot of experience with men's penises. His is about average I'd guess.

I haven't been using anything. Neither has Adam. Says he'll take care of it, then can't remember where he put them and then wow, no time. But I'm not all that regular so it's like dodging bullets.

New Year's Eve but I probably still have time to go to the pharmacy on Division. I need to start behaving like a responsible adult and not a lovestruck ditz.

What time are we meeting Dory? Poking him gently in the ribs.

Seven-thirty. Her place. What time is it getting to be?

I don't know. Sun's off the skylight, so probably it'll be dark soon. Go take your bath.

I'm too comfortable. You go first.

No, you go. You're quicker.

I have the answer. I wash your back, you wash mine. I wash your ears, you wash mine. Then I wash all the good parts and you wash—

Forget it. I just want to lay there up to my chin and have a good soak. Get up, sweet angel. Anyway, you need to go to the liquor store.

Why?

Because we've drunk most of your mother's best stuff, and there's no way we're going empty-handed to Dory's. How far is she?

Upper West Side. Eighty-eighth and West End.

Seven-thirty, you said?

Or thereabout. No rush. All we're going to do is sit around for an hour and reminisce about the glimpses we had of Mom when we were growing up.

That sounds bitter. A note of bitterness.

I think Dory's the bitter one. Mom was just a stiff with kids, that's all, but Dory took it hardest. She gets her revenge on the other celebrities she makes sly fun of in Charisma. *Paparazzi fodder. Bad camera angles, the big noses, the midriff fat on beaches from St. Barts to Juan-les-Pins. Those hordes of living glossies who are already Trivia questions. By the way, Dory's current boyfriend was an alien abductee.*

Is there a lot of that going around?

To hear Dory tell it.

I crept out from under the covers and reached for a robe.

There's nowhere like New York. Are we going to Times Square?

Best place in the world to be on New Year's Eve.

I felt a quick tailspin into a downer mood. Out of nowhere.

If Al Qaeda doesn't pick this time and that place to join the nuclear club.

Security is tighter than a gnat's asshole, Adam said. But we could spend the rest of the night here watching old Twilight Zone *episodes on the SciFi Channel.*

I'm my own Twilight Zone *episode.*

I forgot, Adam said cautiously.

No, let's go to Times Square.

There is a certain edgy appeal to welcoming the New Year while wondering if you're about to be vaporized.

Will you stop? I said—although I'd started it. I want to go to Times Square and be joyously squished with a million other drunkards. But we probably won't be able to get anywhere close.

Leave that to Dory. She's a child of the city. A native Nooyawkah. Whatever it is, she always has tickets. She knows all the entrances and exits, the ins and outs, the subterranean passages, the passwords and secret knocks, the right shoes to wear, getting from here to there with the least amount of bloodshed.

I went to run my bath. Which can take a while, a tub that size. I took care of personal matters in the privy that was outfitted with double commodes and other luxuries, all the fixtures eighteen-karat gold.

When I came out Adam was dressed.

Forgot it was Sunday. But I can probably pick up some wine at the superette before they close, he said.

✦

The huge old freight elevator on our side of the building is slow and noisy. Every sound echoes. At the north end of the old brewery there were other studios, occupied mostly by painters. Occasionally we heard them, their voices echoing too. Everyone used the same elevator and at street level came and went by a single door, which was steel and had good locks.

Even so it creeped me out a little being up there alone, although I knew Adam would be gone for only twenty minutes. I guess Stella Moritz was made of sterner stuff than I was.

But she also had a shotgun convenient to her bed in an umbrella stand. Daddy had one like it. A Remington twelve-guage, the short-barrel model 870. She kept the shotgun loaded with number four buck. Awesome.

If the Remington pump failed her for some reason, she also had a cabinet filled with finely crafted skeet guns, six to ten thousand dollars apiece. She belonged to an exclusive gun club on Long Island.

Every time Adam casually mentioned some new prowess of hers, I felt a little more insecure about meeting Stella Moritz.

I lighted half a dozen aromatic candles on the ledge on the opposite side of the tub and helped myself to bath oils.

I had one foot in the tub when my old pal the Spaz showed up.

Because I was already straddling the tub I decided just to get in and ride this one out while I enjoyed my bath.

Before my other foot went into the water I heard a popping sound. Something struck me in the side like a biting fly.

That was how Crow liked to announce himself when he "came around" from the Netherworld. To use a nonphenomenological term. He couldn't break my nerve so he'd break something else. A makeup mirror, a little *vasa murrhina* of oil. I was supposed to be terrified.

Instead I slipped down into the tub, wary of broken glass. The water came up nearly to my chin. I felt secure in its volume and heat. I had a grip on a bronze bar, although the tub bottom was partially covered with a nonskid mat.

I inhaled moist air. You hick bastard, I said. You worthless spit-tobacco pissjar peckerwood, get away from me.

My eyes were sealed shut. New darkness, familiar flame. His dark figure against the background of fire, twisted, rooted, like a dead tree that refused to fall. That was almost always how it began, the seeing of another place during spells of blindness.

The sound of his voice. Now, then.

Reckon how I do get to missin our little visits, Chase.

My side smarted where a bit of bottle glass had cut me. I'd be bleeding, tinging the bathwater with the color of his vengeance.

He chuckled.

So ye been gittin along okay. Or so it would seem.

Go away you hash-brained baby-raping misfit.

Come on now. You know ye miss me too.

The shit. What I know is I should've killed you myself. Deader than dead and I wouldn't have to be taking this anymore.

My eyes burned behind closed lids. I smelled eternal fire in the Pit near which I had failed to cut his throat.

Hey?

You heard me.

Got somethin all figured out, do ye? Pity ye missed your turn way back then.

He couldn't touch me. We were just crossed-up in a time-and-space warp between dimensions, ricocheting off each other like hostile atoms. But there were things he could do when I was vulnerable to make me suffer. The bathwater was heating up. Crow was angry.

Got ye fixed up with a new boyfriend, hey?

What's it to you.

Nothin. He don't matter none to me.

Then leave us alone and be on your way you prick.

I mean he don't matter no more than some a them other pussy boys you taken up with. Ye ain't tryin too hard to see me, Chase. Ye can try harder if ye be a wantin to.

Oh ha ha. I don't. I don't need to be seeing you, I can still smell you and that's bad enough!

Still got that sass. Remember, Chase? How it was first time we laid eyes on each other? Hell I was doin your mama right fine but then I said to myself this girl, ain't she a looker. This here one is what ye come to this family for, Crow.

God DAMN YOU. Don't you say my mother's name. Don't you talk dirty about her, she has her peace now and I reckon you can't stand that.

What God? Where? Not anywheres I am nor plan to be. No devils neither.

You're the devil.

That water gittin a little too hot for your comfort, missy?

I can take it. I can take any torment you can think of because you don't scare me.

I felt something drip on my forehead. It wasn't water. It wasn't blood. It was viscous and it slid slowly down to an eyebrow and then onto a closed lid. I bit my tongue to keep from crying out.

Crow chuckled again.

What's the matter, little girl? Ye don't have no taste for brains? Them's ain't exactly calf brains, now is they?

The chuckle became the laughter of a madman. I ducked my head under the steaming water to wash his brains off my face. I held my breath for a while, but I could still hear him.

So this new beau a yourn, what's he called?

You know his name.

Hot'n heavy with him air ye? Reckon it be true love this time? Not just one a them boys to kick out a bed when they is done servicin ye?

His mocking tone. His brutal contempt.

Look at me, Chase. While we still got our time together. Look at me and I'll ease up on ye, I swear.

I lifted my head out of the water, gasping, feeling for a washcloth.

Or maybe ye druther see this.

The image that came to my mind was Casey Shields falling over dead after being hit in the chest with a .44 Magnum slug.

Stop it!

Or this.

Mama, lying in her casket. And later times, other funerals. The grief was such a burden on my heart I thought it would explode.

I was your first, and I aim to be your last. Forever.

I felt as if I was being boiled alive. I tried to climb out of the bathtub. One of the silk scrolls wrapped itself around my head and neck and I couldn't move, strangling on erotica. I couldn't breathe. I sat perfectly still, thinking of home. Thinking of my special place by the lake when I wanted to be alone.

Then I could breathe again. I had beaten Crow. But he came at me from another angle, attacking where I was most vulnerable now.

Ain't ye the least curious what I'm thinkin on? What wonders lie in store?

No.

Because ye can't have him and ye can't have it, Chase!

Motherfucker what are you talking about?

This Adam. He was a man a faith once, wa'n't he? Deep in his heart probably got all kinds a faith left. In you. His new religion name a Chase Emrick. Let's put that faith to the test, what d'ye say, Chase?

No! Not this time! This time there's nothing you can do, because together we're stronger than you are!

Well. Reckon we'll see about that.

The water suddenly was draining out of the tub. Making a loud sucking noise. The water had gone from very hot to icy in a matter of seconds.

I peeled the silk scroll from around my neck and as I did so my eyes opened. My teeth were chattering.

Then I saw Crow Tillman. Or I saw the image of a yellow eye like a faint orb of reflected sun, a crack in a pane of skylight glass overhead.

I could cry then. So I had a good one sitting naked and shivering in the empty tub until I heard the freight elevator and knew Adam was coming.

He wasn't going to see me like this. I climbed out of the tub ungainly as a newborn colt and wrapped myself in a terry robe from the warming rack.

By the time he walked in flushed from the cold and with a happy face I was ready to smile. I'd already had some practice at hiding my glooms and shakes from him. Covering the big pulse in the artery of my neck with one hand while I brushed my hair. Hiding the raw truth of the dangerous dilemma I couldn't bring myself to talk about, the shadow-sense of tragedy on my heart.

I thought I understood the powers and treachery of Crow Tillman. But in spite of the horrors he'd brought to me already, I didn't know anything yet.

Adam
December. Last Year.
New Year's Eve.

If there were terrorists about that night in New York they'd made a bad job of things: at two minutes into the New Year most of the kissing and some of the singing were over with and all of us in the vicinity of Times Square were still alive and, perhaps, feeling a sense of relief, depending on one's degree of sobriety.

Chase and I had watched the luminous gold ball descend above the heads of merrymakers chanting down the seconds at Broadway and Forty-second Street from the terrace of a penthouse four blocks north on Seventh Avenue. The top floor of an office building that served as headquarters for *Charisma* and *Bold* and half a dozen other magazines devoted to the hijinks and *Schadenfreude* of the celebrity whirl: movies, TV, fashion, music, publishing. Some of them were on hand for the *Charisma* bash. None were particularly scintillating.

I wasn't either, but Chase stood tall in a silver brocade pantsuit and a necklace of chunky burgundy-and-black beads, all of which I had combined balances on two credit cards to pay for. My belated Christmas present to her, other than roses.

And she had solemnly given to me, an hour before midnight, what I was sure was a prized possession: her father's bronze star from two tours of duty in Vietnam.

"From one brave man to another," she'd said.

I protested. "Chase, this is a keeper. You shouldn't—"

"You're a keeper," she said, looking steadily into my eyes. Her own eyes simmered. She'd had a few, but she was getting good at holding her liquor, even if it was only sauvignon blanc.

"How do you know I'm brave?" I said.

"For one thing, you're a cop."

"Oh, yeah. In mortal danger every day from six thousand maniacal Yale students. You haven't known combat until you've had to break up a Deke kegger."

She smiled slightly.

"You're brave because you made a decision to stick with me. Even though you know I'm haunted."

"I never think about that," I said, which was mostly true. "But if there's a choice I prefer haunted people to haunted castles. Castles are drafty."

"That's funny," Chase said, not smiling this time. "But not particularly. Sometimes you—"

"I know. Anyway, this medal is part of your family's heritage."

"Daddy would have liked you," she said with a glow of remembrance. "And you're my family now."

Although most of the other partygoers were drifting inside out of the cold as the fascination of fireworks over the East River wore off, we stayed on the terrace, a windbreak of arbor vitae in large planters near us, along with one of those outdoor kerosene heaters on a pole. My arms were around Chase.

"Ready to go in?" I asked her, while a sky burst resounded through the Manhattan canyons.

"No, the band's too loud. I'm half deaf already."

"The more tattoos, the lousier the band," I suggested.

"What do they call themselves?"

"Lethal Injection."

"Says it all."

I looked around the terrace. Most of those remaining for the fireworks seemed also to be on cell phones, talking to loved ones or just trying to line up something more interesting for the rest of the night.

"Cell phones," I observed, "are to adults what toy rattles are to infants."

"I have three," Dory's boyfriend said. I hadn't seen him coming. "And a BlackBerry. Couldn't get along without them."

His name was Rod Elbert. Actor on a CBS soap, playing the part of the Juvenile Psycho. Because of his history as an alien abductee, a subject I was sworn never to bring up in his presence, I had expected Rod to be, well, sort of twitchy. Instead there was something more than expressionless about him—his unlined face was static, enduring, like a well-mounted trophy head. He did, however, glance at the sky frequently while on the terrace, and not in the direction of the fireworks display.

Wherever we had been that evening in or around the penthouse Rod had managed to track us down. In his own inscrutable way I think he had developed a crush on Chase.

"Why not?" she'd said, when I mentioned my suspicion, or misgivings to her. And then, with her sometimes perverse sense of humor: "Don't you think we'd make a peach of pair? He's waiting for the mother ship to return, and I've got this nemesis from the Netherworld."

"Never-ending topics of conversation," I agreed.

Rod said, "I've been waiting three months to be on the cover of *Soap Idols*, but now Dory tells me I'm going to be bumped again."

"That's a shame, Rod."

"One million readers. I'm really pissed. Dory says it's out of her hands. Oh." He remembered why he was there. "Dory wanted me to let you know we're leaving for the Waldorf pronto. Pablo Brancusi's party. He's the designer? Raising money for African orphans. Angelina and Brad are rumored to be there. We have a limo waiting."

"My apologies to Dory," I said after a glance at Chase. "We'll just stay around here a while longer, then take the train downtown."

"You should avoid the subway tonight," Rod said. "I've heard rumors."

"I'm sure security is A-number-one."

Rod looked at the sky that was painted with fireworks. His expression changed slightly. He seemed pleased about something. He shrugged.

"Oh, well." An expression of regret that seemed to sum up his worldview. "Vladimir Putin says we're all going the way of the dinosaurs."

"I'm not in a hurry," Chase said. "We'll just take the local."

Rod looked blankly at Chase, said What a pleasure, hope to see you again soon, shook my hand and went off to join Dory in the limousine.

"Whew," Chase said, or breathed.

"Is it just me, or does Rod seem to dispense funk like a disavowed god?" I said.

"Fireworks are about over."

"Want to move on?"

"Straight to bed," she said. "With you."

"You're wearing this dinosaur out."

"But while you're still around, you're lovely in the sack."

For those of you who have never visited New York, or anyone else not familiar with the subway system, I should tell you that the Times Square stations are huge: a maze of long passageways, steep stairs, trackage on three or four levels. There's a connecting link to Grand Central, the shuttle. From Times Square you can travel deep into the Bronx or to the tip of Manhattan. Or out to Queens, Brooklyn, JFK, Far Rockaway and the Atlantic beaches. At Penn Station, one stop below Times Square, you change for the tubes to New Jersey or the Long Island Railroad.

The entire century-old sprawl is muggy and reeking in summer, damp and chilly in winter, dim in places, often dirty, archaeological. The grimy rub of a passing civilization on tile walls, lifestyles of an underground culture. Noisy and jammed at rush hours, with an eerie muffled herd echo and the steely screech of incoming trains, the subway is never deserted. There is a permanent if nomadic twenty-four-hour population: the homeless, the petty lawless, the not quite sane.

I'd gone to public and private schools in Manhattan until I got shipped off to boarding school, and I had ridden the subway almost every day of my New York existence. I loved it all.

✄

Thirty-eight minutes into the New Year.

Revelry from the emptying streets had spilled down into the subway: the joint was jumping. An exuberant crowd. Plenty of party left in their bones. Bottles and beer cans in paper bags. Crowds made Chase queasy, or maybe it was the sauvignon blanc. She squeezed my hand tightly. Noisemakers and tin rattles. Kids sprawled asleep on their daddies' shoulders. There was a three-piece bluegrass band and a guy with a zither and a couple of mimes providing all the entertainment value of a chorus line of post office clerks. Cops patrolled in pairs wearing combat gear and carrying automatic weapons. They looked as if they had heard rumors. Police dogs at turnstiles. Random searches backed up traffic.

Some confusion, milling around. Out-of-towners consulting schedules.

"I know how we got here, but," Chase said.

"Easy. We want the N or the R train—Broadway local. There won't be an express this time of night. Downtown to Canal Street. Transfer there to the J, M, or Z train, get off at Marcy Avenue, the first stop in Brooklyn."

"Oh. So which way now?"

I looked around, not all that sure. "This way," I said finally, gesturing with my free hand.

Kids ambulatory but secluded with their iPods in the fourth dimension called youth. A girl with a petite face was doubled over throwing up in a waste can, her date with an arm around her waist for support. Someone blatted a tin horn in my ear. A group of middle-aged adults in costume. I felt Chase's hand loosen on mine. I was jostled and stumbled. A loose party balloon, silver and red with jellyfishlike paper streamers, grazed my face on its flight to the ceiling.

We came to a wide intersection of passageways, staircases. The earth beneath us rumbled.

"Chase?"

Through the crowd I saw her a little distance away, standing with her back to me.

She was watching three men wearing white shirts, black suits, and crowns of thorns. One of them had an open Bible in one hand. He was reading Scripture but the din was such I could hear only some of his words. Another of the trio had a tambourine he shook to emphasize the preaching. Tears of blood were painted on his cheeks.

The bodies of the gaunt men were twisted, as if all were afflicted by skeletal malformation or arthritic diseases.

The third man was down on his padded knees like the hunchback of Notre Dame shouldering a large wooden cross made of six-by-six beams that looked stained by sweat and body oils, scarred and heavy. His expression confirmed that he was suffering nobly and vicariously from the weight.

I made my way back to Chase. She was about twenty feet from the trio of evangelists.

I caught her hand from behind and she jumped, turned to me with a sickly face.

"Let's get out of here," she said.

"What's wrong?"

"That one," she said with a backward nod of her head as if she didn't want to look around, "the tall emaciated guy. He called me by my name."

I glanced at the preacher with the Bible, a red ribbon that served as a book mark dangling from it like a toad's tongue.

"Do you know him?"

"No!"

He had a hectoring finger poised in the air. His lank black hair hung to his shoulders. His eyes were a particularly disturbing shade of yellow-green, a poisonous shade called Scheele's green, as I recalled from my high school chem lab. Arsenite. They fulminated with the fury of a damning message I half heard.

He glared at me, then leveled that bony white finger at Chase.

"They who commit adultery and walk in lies shall be damned eternally, never to see loved ones again!"

Now wait a minute, I thought, his eyes and manner combusting in my brain, a spreading fever of animosity and recklessness. I could be hotheaded, and I just didn't like seeing this bullshit evangelist polluting the Word of God, no matter my current status as a weak-kneed, spiritually malnourished agnostic.

Chase tried to hold me back, but I left her and pushed my way through a cross-stream of commuters closer to him.

He seemed momentarily to find my interest, hostile as it was, attractive: as if I were the audience he had been seeking tonight.

That close I liked him even less. Those eyes—dog's eyes; a certain malevolent breed, or half-breed, of dog that was still sharp in my memory.

"But everyone shall die for his own sin!" I preached back at him, more or less quoting from Jeremiah. "Each man who eats sour grapes, his teeth shall be set on edge."

He smiled direly at me. He had a head full of old sick teeth from which his lips drew back like a snarling dog's. I was fascinated, wary, sensing emanations, a power of will from a dark place of the universe.

"Adam!" Chase said pleadingly. "Come on!"

The preacher glanced her way. Delight shone in his eyes as if she'd called to him as well, invitingly.

"The Lord will add sorrow upon your pain; ye will be weary with groaning, and find no rest!"

He knew Jeremiah too, although I doubted he had done his master's thesis on that particular book of the Bible, comparing the Hebrew text to the Septuagint.

I scoffed and found a quarter in my pocket, which I flipped contemptuously at his sordid-looking face.

It might have hit him. I don't know. Because at that instant the lights went out.

Not just in the subway but, as we learned later—in my case much later—all over midtown Manhattan.

There was a shocked silence, then an uneasy uproar. Emergency lighting was scarce and slow to come on. But people weren't just standing around waiting for it to happen. In the dark they were shuffling, groping, pushing against one another, raising panicked voices.

I thought I heard Chase calling me. I yelled back: *Over here!* But I couldn't be sure where her voice had come from, as if she unwillingly was being carried away from me by a tide of human flesh, an impulse wave impossible to resist. I had to struggle to hold my own position, stay on my feet.

When there was enough light—Maglites here and there in the hands of cops for the most part—to keep us all from stampeding witlessly, I saw that the space that the three evangelists had occupied was now filled by the milling crowd.

They had packed up their cross and taken their creepy selves elsewhere.

I looked all over. I didn't see Chase. I called her again.

If she'd heard me, I couldn't distinguish her voice in the hubbub. I got stepped on, shoved up against a pillar by a three hundred-pound Hispanic woman.

A metallic voice announced: *Please be calm during this temporary power outage! There is no danger if you remain calm!*

That was greeted with a sort of undulating moan of dread, as the crowd momentarily fell into a suspenseful state of waiting for the rest of the news.

All trains are delayed! Train service at this station will be resumed as soon as possible. (Groan). *Do not attempt to exit the station at this time!* (Alarm). *Do not attempt to cross or walk on the tracks! Power will be restored! Your Metropolitan Transportation Authority wishes you a prosperous and happy New Year.*

The undertone of unease changed to groans of derision, scattered laughter, some profanity. Then almost everyone began moving again in a renewed surge of holiday joie de vivre, ignoring cops trying to keep order. No panic. A fire flared in a wastebasket but that didn't spook them either. The traveling bluegrass band entertained with a plucky banjo-driven "Wildwood Flower." Cell phones were popping open everywhere. Depending on perspective they glowed like fireflies, or benign spirits floating through a Midsummer Night's dream.

Cell phones. They might prove to be the leaded drinking vessels of the day (an analogy I was contrarily pleased with and a reference most people didn't get). But Chase had one and I had mine and apparently we weren't too far underground at this level for my phone to show full bars. I speed-dialed her number.

But Chase didn't answer.

My failed attempt to locate her by phone was when my mood shifted from resigned annoyance to nervous dismay.

Not that Chase wasn't an adult and fully capable of taking care of herself in this modest emergency underground. And I had referred her to the train we'd be taking, although not where to find it.

But—

But, I wondered, how could we have become so totally separated in less than two minutes? Although there were a lot of people, we'd been in complete darkness for only a matter of seconds. Now movement was more purposeful and orderly as stranded commuters got their bearings.

There had not been loud or distant explosions to worry about. We were not beginning to drop like flies from invisible clouds of gas. Therefore it wasn't terrorists at work, at least locally; it was just a New York thing. Unavoidable. Temporary. Trains would be standing partially in or out of tunnels and those trains already parked at their platforms with doors open while waiting on a return of the juice would have their own emergency lighting.

That loudspeaker voice of authority continued to provide

helpful psychic orientation. *You're okay. You're okay. We'll have you all in your beds before you know it. This is a New York thing.*

Somewhere in the cavernous near-darkness of the Times Square subway a woman screamed: a sound filled with such terror as to shrivel the roots of the heart and kick the reptilian brain into overdrive.

The response where I stood was nearly pandemic. No telling just where the scream had come from, but cops were on the move. Incoherent crackle of voices on a couple of walkies. The crowd trembled with the impulse to blind flight.

Chase, I thought. With no reason whatsoever for believing it was Chase who had screamed. But I was trembling too.

My cell phone chimed. I answered.

"Chase!"

She wasn't there. No one was.

The screen, instead of showing me the caller's number, was blank. Then something appeared briefly there, like a streak of dark lightning. Half a second. Barely time enough to register in the mind. But too precise, illustrative, to be a malfunction.

No one could've predicted what consequences a second scream might have had on the flight instinct of those around me. But there wasn't a second scream or hysterical plea for help. Tension began to ebb. Phone conversations resumed. A few smokers were lighting up defiantly to calm their nerves.

I edged toward the stairs I thought would take me to the level where, I hoped, I would find the passage and (as I remembered) another steep flight of steps to the platform and track for the Broadway local.

I went down hugging the wall on my right, tight grip on the railing, along with others who were doing the same. Jostling in the dark. Muttering apologies. Atypical politeness as a form of self-preservation. In a faceless world basic instincts were awry: you had no visual or subliminal clues as to who might be willing to kill you for the most trivial reasons.

Someone a step above tripped and fell against me. I made a lucky grab and managed to keep my balance. She had gin breath.

"Thanks."

"No problem."

"I broke a goddamn heel."

I kept a grip on her until we reached the lower level. She thanked me again and went limping on her way. Leaving her, I had a renewed concern for Chase.

Footsteps. Vague figures passing.

It was quieter down here, not nearly as crowded. Breathing room. Some kids huddled against a wall, passing a toke around. It had been a while since I'd smoked grass. I wished I had some.

I began to call, not loudly.

"Chase? Where are you?"

Other teenagers whom I couldn't see picked up my call and passed it on mockingly, melodramatically: *Chaaaa-aaase!*

Still no answer.

Someone was using a cigarette lighter to study a route map. A child whined.

"Stay close to Daddy."

I came to the last stairway.

Looking down into the lower depths, below which there were no more tunnels or trains, I saw one—faintly aglow from inside the cars, sitting beside the downtown platform.

I took the stairs almost too fast for safety, afraid that this ghostly vision of a train would vanish before I reached the platform.

No one else was on the stairs, going or coming. With most of the station crowd above and behind me, the quiet here was almost unnerving.

As far as I could tell in the available light, which had a bleak luminosity too feeble to cast shadows, the platform was deserted.

The waiting train consisted of only three cars. The one nearest the stairs appeared empty. But I saw movement in the middle car and ran, jumped aboard.

She was sitting with her back to the door at one end of the car.

"Chase!"

"Adam. You made it."

She turned her head as I approached her. I saw that her eyes were tightly closed. There was a look of morbid strain in her face. Her lips were pale and taut.

I sat down and put an arm around her.

"Are they here?" she whispered.

"Who?"

I looked around. The three evangelists and their cumbersome cross were at the front end of the otherwise empty car, sitting in a tight little group wearing their crowns of thorns, blood teardrops on two faces. Only one of the evangelists, the tallest, observed me, his fierce eyes cutting through the dusky gloom.

He reached down with one hand and put something on the floor, gave it a flick with his index finger. I couldn't see what it was. Then I heard it, as it rolled the length of the aisle toward us. In the stillness of the stalled subway car the sound grew from nearly inaudible to the noise a set of iron wheels might make. But it was only a single coin, rolling on edge.

Chase flinched. "They're here, aren't they?"

The coin, a quarter, struck the heel of my boot and spun ringingly on the aisle floor.

"What's that?"

I picked up the quarter. "They gave back my offering," I said.

"You should have left them alone," Chase said worriedly.

"It doesn't matter."

"But it does! Adam, we have to get off this train."

"I don't know who they are," I said. "But I'm not afraid of them. They all look like they got tangled up in airplane propellers."

Her fingers dug into the muscle above my knees.

"I know them," she said. "And maybe we should be afraid."

"Why?"

"Because they're dead," Chase said.

Those three, nobody knew for sure where they'd come from, or cared, at least in the beginning. In my mother Claudelle's time as a child, which was in the middle sixties (and probably now as well), Jubilation, like other north Georgia counties, had a population of roamers, white trash according to some, who drifted down from the mountains to the city, drifted back again on no particular schedule. They were clannish, tightlipped. Traveled in all manner of hard-used trucks and station wagons. Squalid campers piggybacked on pickups, roof racks with household goods in tied-down bundles. As many folks as could be crammed into a camper, never less than six to a wagon, sometimes eight including babes in arms and at least one old granny or pap half blind, tumors, joints filled with the stings of angry bees.

Where there was work they stayed. The men carried mechanic's tools from one jackleg garage to another, patched roofs, dug wells, did county labor if they couldn't stay out of jail. Their women, Mama told me, took any job they could handle with a third or maybe high as sixth-grade education. There were, back then, a few cheap motor court rooms available by the week, or old shotgun houses that families could move into, do fix-up to cover the rent.

And there were churches to welcome them where the style of worship was howl and weep. New Birth Primitive Baptist. Creek Hollow Pentecostal.

Now those three: the ones with the painted-on blood tears, they're brothers. Wes and Roy Gene Curdy. The tall one with yellow-green eyes is their cousin Talis Lawhorn, who only laid claim to being a preacher. He said that he had never read another book but the Bible and maybe half understood some of it. But what he thought he knew made him an apostate. And such men can be dangerous leaders, my father told me (he was battlefield-promoted to captain in Vietnam, and knew about dangerous leaders).

But Talis had an itch to lead. No other pastor's church or preaching could satisfy him for long. In no time at all he could turn a disagreement over the interpretation of a verse from Scripture into a schism, then a blood feud where the flock was forced to take sides.

So it was that the pastor of Balm of Gilead Holiness, Bob Eggleston, found himself hopelessly on the outs with Talis and his clan. After due process and a vote among the elders of Balm of Gilead, Pastor Bob excommunicated the bunch of them, women and children included.

Talis promptly started his own storefront church, with nearly half of the congregation from Balm of Gilead tagging along, but he and the Curdy brothers weren't finished with Pastor Bob.

(Daddy told me the rest of their story when I was eight or nine and the murder of Bob Eggleston two decades ago was still fresh in the minds of a lot of people in Jubilation County. I'd heard some of it whispered to me by a cousin at a brush arbor meeting who had pointed out a woman she said was a stepdaughter of Roy Gene Curdy.)

Pastor Bob and "Pastor" Talis had been naming each other Satan for a few weeks, a terrible business that shook the souls of grown men and frightened children, because there's probably no one in Jubilation County even today who doesn't take Satan seriously, blaming him for every flat tire, miscarriage, or dark cloud that appears in the sky.

Talis Lawhorn and the Curdy boys settled the question of who was right about the Satan thing by paying a call on Bob around sunset of an August day. They arrived unannounced carrying shotguns and walked in. Pastor Bob was a slight man, thin of bone and hair, thirty-something and unmarried. He lived with his old parents in the house where he'd been born and was reading the Atlanta Journal in his study where he had a small window air-conditioner going.

His dinner came up all over his shirtfront when the three assassins appeared and took stances on three sides of Bob's chair. They all had shooter's plugs in their ears.

According to the best recall of Bob's old daddy—who happened to be in the hall bathroom nearby with the door slightly ajar in case he took a fall getting up off the toilet—when Bob had cleared his throat and could speak he said, If I am going to be murdered by you trash, I want to be standing on my feet giving great praise to my Lord and Savior Jesus Christ.

His very Name is profane upon your lips was Talis Lawhorn's response. Then they slaughtered Pastor Bob where he sat in his La-Z-Boy, three shotguns firing at once.

Talis and the brothers walked out of the Eggleston house as they had come in, a mess of blood themselves because the late Pastor Bob's study was on the small side.

They drove in Wes Curdy's pickup to the storefront church where the congregation was waiting, standing wall to wall. Talis gave them the news. There was moaning and weeping. On her knees in front of the pulpit Talis's wife Truly rent her garments and tore at her hair. Their three small children danced as if they were barefoot on hot plates and fell in fits to the floor.

Talis took this in beatifically and with upraised hands. He told the congregation that it should be the good Lord who judged the worth of what he and the Curdy brothers had done. As many among them had *suspected, was Pastor Bob evil incarnate? Talis proposed a trial by strychnine. If he and the Curdys swallowed deadly poison and survived, then their blood action surely must be deemed righteous in the eyes of their Creator.*

Amens to that.

The assassins swallowed strychnine, a load of it. Each was stone dead inside of ninety seconds, their joints pulled apart from stressful doomed thrashings, when sheriff's deputies moved in to make arrests.

"Killed themselves and went straight to hell," I said. "Metaphorically speaking."

"Let's not do metaphors right now."

"Okay. Ashes to ashes, dust to dust. A grave is a grave forever. So if those guys sitting up front in their wearing-out shoes and needing baths are Talis what's-his-name and the Curdy brothers, how do you—?

"That's just it," Chase said. "No hell, whatever it may be, for them. And death by suicide isn't death yet. Suicides are unfinished lives. There's no final reckoning. Suicides all wind up in the Netherworld for sorting out, processing by—I don't know. Maybe there's a committee. But the Netherworld is where Crow could have rounded up those three and sent them out again. To us."

"To do what? You said Tillman is bound by some immutable law over yonder that keeps him at least arm's length from you."

"Yes."

"So if Crow has emissaries, aren't they subject to the same law?"

"Not where you're concerned."

"Shit can happen, you mean."

"And does. And has, if you've been paying attention."

"I've been awarded a bronze star for bravery."

"Don't mock."

I had another quick look at the three men. I wasn't laughing, but in spite of my own brief experience with Crow Tillman I wasn't taking her seriously either.

"They look pretty solid to me. As solid as the old rugged cross they're hauling around."

"Solid? Okay, go up there and give one of them a poke."

"Uh-uh. They'd probably take it the wrong way. I'm brave but that doesn't make me a fool for hard times."

"Adam—when you got here did you see a, what d'you call them, a driver for this train? Or a conductor, or—are we all by ourselves?"

"Apparitions excluded."

"Shut up. So there isn't anyone else on board?"

"So far."

"Sweet angel, I want off this train. Right now."

I didn't argue. I was feeling edgy myself, maybe from a sense I was being stared at, those yellow-green eyes fixed on the back of my head.

"You don't want to wait until—"

"No. Please help me up."

All three men followed our progress to the open door, with varying degrees of interest. The two brothers—if they were brothers—put their heads together, conferring. The preacher gave me a last look and opened the Bible in his lap.

"Okay, watch your step here," I said to Chase.

There was an intense flare of light inside and outside the subway car. It seemed to be composed of concentric rings expanding—I had no better way to describe the phenomenon—each ring more brilliant than the last. I didn't know where the flash had come from. It might have been centered near the preacher's bowed, thorn-cinctured head. But the shock of it had distorted my senses. I felt sharply nauseated.

Although I didn't hear an explosion, the train lurched violently. I kept my grip on Chase as she fell against me and grabbed a pole for support.

"WHAT HAPPENED?" Chase said, her voice low but with the intensity of a scream.

"I don't know. Maybe the power—" I said, as the punishing light shrank to a mote in my brain and the deep dusk we'd been accustomed to prevailed.

But the door slid shut as I was about to guide Chase ahead of me onto the platform. The train lurched again, then smoothly began to enter the tunnel.

"We're going?" she said with a pleased smile. "The power's back on?"

"Must be. We couldn't budge without juice to the third rail."

"Then—what's wrong?"

"Wrong? Nothing. Why don't we sit down again?"

As the subway train picked up speed and began a rocking motion I put her in a seat closest to the door. But I remained standing, protectively, over Chase. Full power still hadn't been restored in our car. Or the other two cars that made up the train, as far as I could tell.

We hit a rail junction and coasted; what lighting there was flickered into deep black. Chase, of course, wasn't aware of the change. She didn't say anything.

The train swayed as it picked up momentum.

When a glimmer of light returned to the car I looked again at Chase.

She wasn't there. The seat was empty.

What is it you got there? I said to one of the brothers. I don't know which one but what did it matter? He held it up for me by the heels so I could see. A newborn baby boy, not a minute old and still covered in afterbirth, with a dangle of purple umbilical like a second snaky penis. Its eyes were clotted closed, but its red mouth was open and I heard a thin pitiful cry. Just-born and wanting, needing its mother.

I had trouble keeping my feet in the tempestuous, jarring unseen world around me.

Give it to me, I said. He's mine and I want him!

Ye can't have it, Crow says.

GIVE HIM TO ME! I screamed. I've had enough of Crow's dirty dealings!

Instead he turned toward the Pit and raised high my child to cast him upon the roasting coals.

Again I screamed.

This time for Adam.

✧

There was no one in the car but myself and the preacher. The other evangelists and Chase had vanished. Yet I heard her scream.

The preacher raised his eyes slowly from the Book and looked at me.

"Where is she, you son of a bitch!"

His sly smile destroyed what rationality I still possessed and, berserk, I went after him, climbing over the barrier cross in the aisle, smearing my hands with blood as I did so, to get hold of his skinny throat.

As I seized him to shake that smile from his lips there was a stir in his nest of greasy hair and the crown of thorns he wore came to life, wrapping itself around my left wrist. I felt a deep sting. Looking away from his smirking face I saw the head of a rattlesnake, half the size of my fist, as the snake drew back atop his skull for another strike.

This time it went for my heart.

From the wheels of the train sparks showered upward. We rocketed through another station as I fell back across a seat on the other side of the aisle, grappling with the now six-foot canebrake rattler, one of the most lethal of its kind.

Chase screamed again.

In the dim light I had a glimpse of her standing in the aisle at the other end of the car. Her eyes appeared to be open. If she was looking at me she didn't react to my predicament and that thrashing bastard of a snake.

"Chase, make it stop!" I yelled. I meant the train. But she didn't respond.

All the lights came on then. After twenty minutes of near-darkness it was suddenly bright as noon. I looked again at Chase. Behind her there was a face, a black guy in a conductor's cap, looking into our car from the one behind it.

It wasn't much of a surprise to me that the advent of light had flushed the third evangelist from the car. Nothing of them remained but the wooden cross. And the rattlesnake I couldn't let go of.

I glanced from its round virulent eyes to the puncture wounds just above my left wrist. I felt a heaviness in my chest where the monster also had struck me. I was scared and short of breath and there was pain like a live wire buried in my poisoned arm.

"Adam?" Chase said, shaking her head and wincing, as if she'd just walked out of one nightmare and into another.

Behind her the conductor opened the door to our car.

"Sweet Mary of Christ! What you doing there with that snake? Ain't real, is it?"

"It's real and it bit me, twice, and unless you get this train stopped and me into an ambulance I'm going to die! God damn it, get a cop to shoot the snake, and get me some help!"

Chase
The New Year.

The detective wearing the brown suit said to me, "We could look it up, but I'd say your boyfriend is the only rider in the history of the New York City subway system ever got bit by a rattlesnake."

There were two of them. Middle-aged. Just ordinary-looking guys. Heavy on the New Yorkese when they spoke. One standing, one sitting next to me, writing in his pocket notebook. Gray suit, brown suit. I had forgotten their names as soon as they told me. I couldn't hold much of anything on my mind, or my stomach. I just wanted them to go away.

A nurse's aide in a colorful smock brought me some Pepto-Bismol in a little paper cup. I thanked her and drank it down.

We had a corner of the waiting room of the Emergency Department at St. Vincent's Hospital to ourselves. Otherwise it was a full house with dawn still a couple of hours away. Outside in the ambulance bay a light bar was flashing in my eyes whenever I looked up. For the most part I kept my eyes on the bronze star case I was holding in my lap.

The gray suit detective said, "That's 3.8 million riders a day. On average. Of course we've had a few alligator sightings."

I looked at him. "I'm sorry. What was your name?"

"I'm Vito. He's Abe."

Abe was looking back a couple of pages in his notebook.

"This Blepharospasm, kind of a rare thing one of the docs told me. He'd never seen a case."

I shrugged.

"So you were temporarily blind most of the time while you were on the train. You can't describe the preachers Adam says were onboard with you."

"That's right. Have you found the snake?"

"Not yet. If it's still hidin' on the train we'll come across it. Otherwise it probably disappeared into the tunnel."

"Like those preachers which by the way the conductor don't remember seein'," Vito said. He was staring at me.

"They shouldn't be all that hard to find," I said, "if they do their preaching in subways."

"We'll probably get something useful, prints maybe, off that cross they left behind."

I nodded again. The nurse's aide came back to me.

"He's asking for you."

"Can I go?" I asked the detectives.

"Sure," Abe said. "We'll need a statement from you, but it

can wait a few hours and maybe you'll think of something else that could help. A name you overheard. We'll give you a call later today, you can come by the squad at your convenience. We're just a couple blocks from here."

The nurse's aide took me back to where Adam was, curtained off from the rest of the night's casualties. A doctor who was our age was conferring with a male nurse.

They had Adam on antibiotics, painkiller, fluids. He wasn't completely knocked out yet but he didn't blink or move his eyes when I put a hand on his shoulder and spoke his name.

"Cold," he said.

I made myself look at his right arm. It seemed likely he was going to lose a part of it, at least below the elbow. The forearm, swollen to twice the normal size, looked as if someone had taken a blowtorch to it. His fingers were swollen too, and purple. There was dead tissue already.

That goddamn snake. I wiped my eyes with the back of a wrist.

The doctor looked over at me. He had curly hair and a pink Irish mug. He was at that stage of sleeplessness where he blinked a lot in order to focus. He'd probably been awake for thirty hours.

He took me aside. I didn't have to ask.

"Too early to tell about the arm. God knows how we happened to have a supply of rattlesnake antivenin in house. But that's a break could make all the difference." He looked at the bronze star case in my hand. "Where did he get that? Iraq?"

"It was my father's. Vietnam, 1971."

"Another lucky break. From the venom on Adam's—it's Adam, right?—from the quantity of venom that soaked into his shirt, if the snake's fangs had reached his heart instead of being deflected by the plastic case in his pocket, he would'na lasted more than two minutes."

"Lucky break," I said dully. "What are you giving him for the pain?"

"Palladone. Around here it's called 'hospital heroin.' He'll be needin' strong stuff for a few days."

I went back to the bed, leaned over Adam. Touched his face. He still felt cold. His lips were dry. I asked a passing nurse for an extra blanket.

"Did I miss the Super Bowl?" Adam said unexpectedly.

"What? I—don't know. Don't they play the Super Bowl like, in February?"

He licked his dry lips. I gave him a little ginger ale to sip through a straw.

"What day—is this?"

"Still the first of January."

"Oh." He didn't say anything else for a while. I thought he might finally be out, but his eyes weren't quite closed. "Peyton Manning," he said.

"Who?"

"Best quarterback—in the NFL. Has a bad day—he'll still beat you. Good day—he'll murder you."

"Hooray for Peyton Manning."

"Got to—make a football fan out of you."

"Good luck trying," I said.

"Hey, Chase?"

"Yes, sweet angel."

"They gonna—let me keep my arm?"

"Oh yes. Hundred percent. But it'll be a little while healing. Don't worry."

I didn't say anything about multiple skin grafts, inevitable disfigurement.

"Worried—about you."

"I'm fine. I called your sister. She's on her way down, you know, from the Waldorf."

"Did they—kill the snake?"

"Couldn't find it."

I saw him flinch slightly, swallow hard.

"It'll come back—then, won't it?"

"No. Never. Don't you believe it."

"Was Crow. Wasn't it?"

"Who thought this one up? Yes. I'm sure."

"Listen. I think—got this guy figured out."

"You what?"

"Ol' Crow's—playing rough. But I can play rough too."

I kissed him. Trying for a little of my magic, if there was any left. It seemed to relax Adam, but my heart was beating too fast. As we say down home, my blood was riz.

"You don't know what you're saying! Oh, baby—what have I *done* to you?"

I had to locate the bathroom again, and fast. I got there in time. Nothing much came up this time. So it was panic, nerves, or something else I'd begun to suspect. I had to almost put my fist in my mouth to keep the hysterics back.

When I returned to Adam, Dory had arrived, on uppers it quickly became apparent, and found him. But Adam was asleep at last.

Dory was slim, dark, a big-eyed girl with the kind of slap-dash haircut that takes about three hours at the hairdresser's to get right. She was up to her earlobes in glossy fur.

"I didn't get Stella but I got her assistant," Dory said. "Apparently Mom is somewhere in the English countryside. Riding to hounds or some shit like that."

"I'm sure she'll be on the first plane back here."

"I have to fly to L.A. in a few hours. Purgatory with palm trees. When Mom does show up, tell her she's not getting off lightly in my memoirs." Dory was going to have permanent wrinkles at a young age for making dour faces. She hugged me then. Hard enough so I could tell she had a body under all that fur. "What are the doctors saying? This is so fucking bizarre." She glanced at Adam's swollen arm. "Who carries rattlesnakes around on the subway? But that's New York. Crackpots and looney tunes. So you take the good with the bad, is what I tell people."

I explained everying I knew about Adam's prognosis.

"God, I'm so worried! But it looks as if he's going to sleep for a while. Join me for a smoke outside?"

"I don't smoke."

"Ever try dip? It's getting to be a thing. Up here."

"Shoot, I gave up dip in second grade."

Dory had to mull that over to find the humor. Someone in another cubicle screamed and Dory jumped. Her flawlessly veneered teeth were on edge.

"I *hate* hospitals. Bet you could use something to eat, chance to lay your head down for a couple of hours. C'mon back to my place with us, I'm making breakfast for the gang. I'll tell you what Bono said about the candid cover we did on him for *Bold*. Rock stars, they're all like women when it comes to their looks. I told him 'Those extra pints, they go right to your chinline, luv.' "

Like I cared. I begged off, saying that I just wanted to stay with Adam.

Dory gave me one of those sympathetic sisterhood-in-distress looks and another embrace. Making eye contact this time. Okay, Dory, I get it.

"Keep us posted. Oh, do I have your cell?"

I gave her the number.

⚡

I spent the rest of the night sitting in a plastic shell of a chair beside Adam. They weren't about to let him out of the hospital. When they found a bed for him in Critical Care I went along too.

I didn't want to leave him alone for even five minutes, but by mid-morning I was foggy and nodding off, of no use to Adam or myself. He was out, as far out as they dared put him, but in spite of the medication he wasn't completely walled off from the pain. He made occasional sounds of distress.

His mother called the hospital, and her call was transferred to the unit. They came and got me.

"Who's this?"

"My name is Chase Emrick, ma'am. I'm—a friend of Adam's, and—"

"Oh yes, Dory told me about you. She didn't mention you were *Southern*. Are you a Georgia peach or an Alabama belle?"

"I'm from Georgia."

"I am *so* looking forward to meeting you. But your nerves. You must be exhausted at this point. I know I would be. Now tell me about this rattlesnake, Chase."

I explained, leaving out dead people.

"They aren't going to have to amputate any part of his arm, are they?"

"I don't know yet." I started to cry then.

"Oh, that's all right, that's all right," Stella Moritz said soothingly. "You simply have to get yourself some rest. I'm sure they're all taking excellent care. Have you been staying with Adam at the loft?"

"Yes, ma'am."

"Hm. I'm trying to recall if I made the bed before I left."

"Everything—was just perfect when we—"

"Listen, Chase—is that a family name? It's darling. The reason I'm not on a plane to New York this minute, I'm being deposed later this week in an embezzlement case involving a longtime friend and business associate who had a psychotic break and made off with tens of thousands of English pounds that belonged to yours truly. Oh." She heaved a transatlantic sigh that made me want to yawn. "It feels like I've been gone forever. And I'm still not sure when—someone in my New York law firm will check with the St. Vincent's administrator today. If there's anything you need, call them. And do you have my current cell? No? Write it down, please." While I was writing she added, "There's no need for hourly bulletins, but if— you know. A turn for the worse."

"Yes," I said, still crying but making an effort to keep it from her.

"You sound lovely. Dory told me you were a world-class mathematician. So like Adam, not to be intimidated by a brainy woman."

Stella Moritz was one of those people who hang up without saying good-bye.

I went back to the loft with Adam's keys, went upstairs in that groaning elevator that was about half the size of a squash court, and collapsed on the waterbed. Feeling a little spooked by the size and lonesomeness of the shadowy loft, the noises in the mews below that I hadn't paid attention to before with Adam there. But I soon fell asleep.

✦

When I sleep I dream a lot, and after waking up I have vague memories of what I've dreamed about. Usually it has to do with being in a strange place and in a hurry to get somewhere else by plane or train or a Jeep Wrangler with one side door missing like Casey Shields had. There were always problems. The plane couldn't fly because it had no wings. The train would turn into a submarine or a carnival ride that went around and around to nowhere. When I finally got off I was eight years old and my mother or father had tired of waiting for me and I couldn't find them. You know those dreams. You have them too. You wake up with a deep sense of grief, of loss, of failure.

It's a curious thing. I had earned them, but I never had nightmares. The really dreadful, wake-up-screaming stuff.

Because, I suppose, I still had Crow Tillman.

Worse than Crow it didn't get.

After seventy-two hours Adam was released from the hospital and I brought him back to the loft in Williamsburg.

By then we knew he wasn't in danger of losing part of his arm or a finger, but he would be needing skin grafts. The swellings had lessened but the arm still looked grotesque. The slightest touch was agonizing to him. Adam was stoic about the pain, but the medication, although reduced, had him docile, a little dreamy, and very loving.

Neither of us was ready or willing yet to discuss what had happened in the subway. And I had another important matter on my mind.

Friday morning I went with Adam to St. Vincent's outpatient clinic, where they put him under and got rid of more dead tissue. We went back to Brooklyn in a cab. His dressings had been changed and his arm was in a sling. Only the tips of his fingers, which were nearly black, showed.

Saturday he felt okay to go for a walk, and he wanted to have lunch at Peter Luger's, a famous old Brooklyn steakhouse.

The weather had turned milder and sunny, mid-fifties during the day. We browsed in the boutiques and used bookstores and tiny galleries on North Sixth, then walked south on Bedford. His stamina was improving. Our reservation at Luger's was for one-thirty. We sat on a bench outside a playground beneath the bridge approach and watched the kids on swings and slides.

"I flunked my EPT test," I said. Out of the blue. I couldn't think of a better way to break the news to him.

He looked at me for ten or fifteen of the longest seconds of my life.

"We were meant to have children," he said.

"Oh, God, I hope so."

"It happened the night we met," Adam said with an incisive nod.

"I know it did," I said. "I was going to say. But I thought you would think I was being mystical."

"What shall we name her, Chase?"

"Not so fast. At this point all we have is a teaspoonful of— her?"

"I want a girl. Don't you think 'Absinthe' is an underused name for girls?"

"With good reason."

"Or how about—'Asphodel?' Or is that a town in New Jersey?"

"Adam, you're druggy."

"Never felt better."

"We could name her after your mom."

"That would be catering to her grandmotherly instincts, of which I'm pretty sure she is completely without."

"Dear God. Your mother. What is she going to think of me? Getting pregnant on my first date? Which wasn't even a date, come to think of it. You practically kicked my door down with an armload of Thai food that wasn't all that wonderful. But please don't think I'm ungrateful."

"Now you tell me. I could have stopped at the Doodle for burgers instead."

With a little smile Adam rested his head on my shoulder.

"Rosebuddd," he whispered.

Sunday morning bright and early Stella Moritz called from the VIP lounge of British Airways at Heathrow. She was coming home.

That sent me into a frenzy of housekeeping. I was determined that when she walked off the freight elevator into her loft there wouldn't be a speck of dust (the walls of the old factory breathed dust) or an unwashed teacup anywhere.

Adam watched a football game on TV, occasionally snarling

in disgust at a fumble or dropped pass. I felt excluded by his fix-ation.

"Maybe we should check into a hotel," I said to him, aware of a note of pleading in my voice. "For a couple of days until she gets settled back into her routine. Then we can, like, come around for a proper visit."

"How much money do I have left?"

I looked into his wallet.

"Thirty-six, no, thirty-seven dollars."

"How much do you have?"

"Emergency stash? Sixty-five dollars."

"Hotel? We're Salvation Army material. Soup kitchens. It's a good thing I'm still drawing a paycheck on sick leave. But the next one isn't due until—"

"Wait. I didn't tell you. I have this 1916 twenty-dollar gold piece my father gave me, just in case. I've held on to it through thick and thin—mostly thin—but today—"

"Keep holding." Adam got out of his chair during a com-mercial break. "Your nose is dirty." He cleaned it for me. "Don't stress out. You've already met Mom on the phone a couple times."

"But Adam. She'll be here in the flesh. A legend. Fully pre-pared to disapprove. Don't tell me any different. Your mother and I are women. And you just wouldn't get it."

"Everybody's a legend in the Arts nowadays. Mostly it's a matter of longevity. Have we completely run out of drunken, forgotten failures? Speaking of which, I could use a beer."

"All out. But I'm going to the store, soon as I finish the tub.

A woman doesn't want to find another woman's pubic hairs in her bathtub."

"If you lean over any farther, you'll fall in and get a concussion."

I took a last swipe with the cleaning sponge and stood up, giving my lower back a stretch, looking over my shoulder at him.

"Adam, don't sit on the bed. Sit in your chair."

"What's the matter with the bed?"

"I just fixed it! Ye gods. Just thought of something. Ye gods."

"Now what?"

"Adam, we've made love in your mother's bed. She'll *know*."

"Are you having a nervous breakdown?"

"Yes."

"We'll go right on sleeping in Mom's bed. She'll want us to. She'll move into that part of the loft that's for overnight guests she's either not in love with or who may be too drunk to put out on the street."

Going down in the slow elevator, Adam said, "We should get married. We keep putting it off."

"We've known each other exactly, let's see, make it twenty-three days tomorrow."

"Are you a Democrat or a Republican?"

The elevator stopped with the ponderous dignity of an elephant kneeling.

"I hate questions where I only have a fifty-fifty chance of being right."

"It's a trick question."

"Hate those too. I'm a strict logician."

"Forget about politics," Adam said as we walked outside. "If we're going to be married, I *will* need a sample of your handwriting. We'll honeymoon for a month in Bali."

"On whose nickel?"

"My mother has accumulated enough frequent flyer miles to send us to Alpha Centauri."

I looked at him on the street. He smiled, but his forehead was creased and his eyes were tight, with a gleam of opiates in the pupils.

"Go back upstairs and lie down," I told him. "I know how to find the supermarket. It's on Broadway, right?"

⚹

So I had Garth Brooks for company on my iPod walking to the market while Adam nursed a rebound headache from painkillers.

At that time—it was three-twenty in the afternoon—I hadn't been away from Adam for more than a few minutes. I'd fed him, bathed him, read to him. If it wasn't for the fact that his mother was en route I wouldn't have left him then. Skipped the marketing and warmed up some leftovers. But I wanted to fix a nice candlelight supper for Stella Moritz, the best I could afford with our shrinking resources.

Okay, it was intended to be an offering. I had a goddess to propitiate, or so I felt.

(See how good I am with the pots and the skillets and the down home vittles? Yes'm, I surely can take right fine care a your manchild, Miss Stella honey.)

That made me laugh as I walked, and I found myself thinking of home, the way it had been before the dark times, Mama and me in the kitchen on a holiday or other special occasions while she taught me how to braise short ribs, marinate wild fowl after we got all of the lead pellets out of the meat, season poultry or pumpkin squash just right.

Mama had never looked at a cookbook in her life. Her side of the family, the women all just naturally knew their way around a kitchen.

I was still deep in sweet and sad reminiscing and a block away, listening to "Beaches of Cheyenne," when I became peripherally aware of the young blind girl standing near the curb in front of the supermarket.

The girl looked to be nine or ten years old. She was wearing a cute blue-and-black plaid coat with matching blue tam and muffler. She carried a white cane with a red tip, a cane that she was tapping on the sidewalk, turning around slowly as if undecided about which direction to go.

As far as I could tell there was no adult with her. She attracted glances from everyone passing by, going into and coming out of the supermarket. She didn't seem disturbed about being by herself. Her blind eyes were a deep overcast shade of brown.

I stopped near her, taking out my iPod earpiece.

"Are you waiting for someone?"

She turned her head quickly when I spoke and smiled happily in my direction.

"You," she said.

"Excuse me?"

"You'd be Chase, wouldn't you?" She had the accent I'd had as a child. As familiar to me as Southern nights, Southern wind. The call of whip-poor-wills. I felt momentarily nostalgic. Over the years I'd lost much of the vernacular due to an excess of education and some of the languid, velvety vowel sounds. The lazed and playful intonation. I was a grown-up now. So to speak.

"Do I know you?"

"I'm Emma," she said. "Emma Pierce, from down Gainesville way?" She laughed and held out her ungloved hand. "No, we couldn't never a met. You was born in '81, wasn't you?"

Her cane tapping, tapping gently on the sidewalk in front of me. Her upturned face serene. I felt a stricture in my breast when I drew a sharp breath.

"Wasn't you?"

"Yes."

"Welll. It was in '68, you see, that Brother'n me was playin in Daddy's brand new pickup? Brother, he was actin like a big shot, pretendin how's he could drive. Turnin the lights on, blowin the horn. Turned the engine on too, left it runnin. The garage closed up. But I'd forgot about that. The garage door bein closed I mean? I was born blind, how it was. Reckon that's no excuse though. I was a year older'n Brother. Should a had my wits about me. But you couldn't hear nor feel the engine runnin. So we was just settin up there in the cab with a bag of pork rinds and two Orange Crushes listenin to the radio, havin us a *good* time. Andddd—it was maybe three hours, four hours that Daddy and Mama turned up, home late from the ball game in Atlanta?"

Emma shrugged. End of story.

Traffic going by in the street was like a blur to me. My senses seemed outlandishly warped, as if I were high on something. A black-and-white dog on a leash gave me a sniff but backed off from Emma Pierce with a scared whine, tail between its legs. People came and went and I stared into her fixed netherworldly eyes. Her baby-tooth smile, gum space, new big ones poking in at angles.

"Oh my God what *is* this?"

"Oh," she said with a little gesture, *"you* know. You're s'posed a take me with you now. In there."

I looked at the supermarket. A boy was loading a delivery bike in front. Inside, the checkout counters were busy. Comings and goings on a bright winter afternoon.

I looked again in wonder at Emma Pierce, stock-still but tapping with her cane, nervous now.

I went down on one knee beside her and put a hand on the hand that held the cane.

"Emma," I said, "honey, you don't have to do this. Whatever Crow Tillman has put you up to, you can stop now. I want you to stop. Please."

She tensed. Her eyes were like round dormant seeds that will never know their season. They couldn't change, but there was confusion in the set of her little mouth.

"No. You hafta come with me," she insisted.

"Why, Emma? What's in the store? Is Crow Tillman waiting in there?"

"Nooo! He can't come his ownself. Said you knowed that. That's why he ast me to come in his stead."

Her lips had disappeared. Her chin was bunched. Her eyelids trembled.

"Don't cry," I said.

"He said—wasn't no way you'd be scairt a *me!*"

"I'm not, Emma. I'm not. But Crow and me—there's this thing, a bad thing happened between us that you don't know about. Oh, he can talk all sweet and friendly, especially to young girls, but—"

"You got a come! You got a see it! I *prom*ised I'd bring you."

"See what?" I said, susceptible to her childish will.

"I don't knowww. It's in the store! That's the way I come here, and how I need to go back. Through the store. But if you won't come with me"—now the tears—"don't reckon as how I can *get* back! Then where will I be? What will I do?"

"Take it easy, Emma."

"Then help me, why'n't you?"

I blotted her cheeks with a tissue. She continued to complain.

"I just don't like it here! It's too noisy. Ever 'body's in such a big hurry. And I'm cold. It's *never* cold back there."

"Back where?"

"Home," she said. "Onlyyyy—not *quite* the way it was. When Brother and me was a-livin. But—it's still okay, reckon."

"You'll go back," I said.

"You swear?"

"I swear."

"You'll take me?"

"No. I can't go there, honey. I'm just not ready."

She nodded dejectedly.

"He said you'd say that. But he also said—wellll, that you didn't really *mean* it? Anyhow I was only talkin about inside the store. You can take me there okay."

"Yes," I said. "I'll go with you. That far. I had some shopping which I'd better get done."

I gave Emma a kiss. She smiled again, a big smile. I envied her dimpled cheeks.

"Let's go then," I said, and took Emma by the hand as I stood. I was curious now. And there were dozens of people in the supermarket. I wasn't afraid. But like forgetful little Emma in the garage with the door closed, I should have known better.

✳

When Emma and I entered the supermarket lobby there was nothing unusual to hear or see. The Muzak selection was instantly forgettable, soap bubbles for the ears. A couple of boys in store aprons were on ladders stapling up specials for the coming week on a banner with red and blue plastic pennants.

A female employee announced in her Brooklynese accent, "*Don't forget to take advantage of Alpha Beta's promotions and sales! Today only, holiday hams, fully cooked, are seventy-nine cents a pound while they last. Twelve packs of Coca-Cola are on aisle six for only $2.99 each.*"

"Emma, where am I taking you?"

"Ought'n you get us a cart?"

I wasn't as focused on shopping as I'd claimed to be, but I took a cart that had a bad wheel from the in-store corral.

"Could I ride, please?" Emma said. "I'm *so* tired. Besides, that wheel would stop a-squeakin if I was to sit in the cart."

"How do you know?"

She didn't say anything else. I gave Emma a lift up to the child's seat in the cart. She was small for her age; even so she could barely squeeze into the seat space intended for preschoolers. She held her white cane vertically.

"This is *fun*," she said. "Bein with you, Chase. Wisht we could always be together."

This girl could wheedle.

"Did Crow tell you to say that, Emma?"

Her lips disappeared again.

"I like you better when you're bein *nice*."

"I like you best, sweetie, when you're not being tricky."

"I'm not!"

"Okay, let's just forget it. Where do I take you now?"

"Just push. We'll find out." Her tone subdued now.

We went into the store. Emma had been right. The wheel stopped squeaking.

"Be sure and take advantage of Alpha Beta's bakery specials. Parker House rolls, only a dollar-ten for a package of twelve. English muffins—"

"Look, Emma," I said to the pouting girl. "I want you to do something for me when you . . . get back. Don't go near Crow Tillman again. He can't make you, so just ignore him. Emma?"

"All right," she said, in a small tearful voice.

In one of the checkout lanes an elderly Jewish woman was arguing about the price of cat food. When her equally old husband or companion nudged her she stopped talking and looked slowly around at us with pink-lidded lashless eyes.

"McIntosh apples, special purchase, are on sale now in our produce department—"

I was looking at Emma, who was mute and downcast, although she had reached up with her free hand to take hold of the front of my coat.

"You're tallll."

"Emma, you know what it is I'm supposed to see. Don't you?"

"—California strawberries—"

"Yes."

"I'm stopping right here until you—"

"Nooo!"

She wasn't loud. But other heads were turning, slowly. It seemed as if everyone in the store had become aware of us. There was a sudden stillness after Emma's plea. The teenage boys on the ladders looked down. It was as if someone had blown a dog whistle at obedience school. But the pitch of this whistle was meant only for the ears of the shoppers and staff of the market. Business had come to a standstill. Emma was oblivious but I felt my cheeks starting to burn from the scrutiny we were getting.

Not that the stares were unfriendly. There was a quiet lack of emotion in all their eyes, a slackness to their faces that unnerved me. As if they were professional mourners, and I was a Jane Doe funeral.

"Emma," I said, "please let go of my coat. I'm getting out of here right now."

"You can't," she pleaded, but she released her grip on me. "Listen."

"What you're looking for," said the woman who had been talking about Alpha Beta's specials over the store's PA system, "can be found down aisle two, Chase. In our meat department."

"Fuck . . . this," I said, and turned back to the doors to the lobby.

The doors were open, but there was no way to get through them. At least a dozen customers and supermarket clerks were filling the doorways, all of them looking at me.

"Our special today," said the coaxing voice, "is very, very special indeed. Chase, you don't want to miss it."

Obviously I wasn't to have a choice. I turned back unwillingly, a volume of dread increasing, exerting pressure on me.

I heard squeaking carts. I turned and looked. About six of them, mothers and fathers pushing, kids in the child seats or in the carts themselves. Coming at Emma and me as a phalanx—I assume you'd call it—blocking the entire front of the market from the checkout lanes to the opposite wall with the ATM and food-for-the-hungry barrels.

"*It's all for you, Chase,*" the nasal voice said. "*Aisle two. The meat department. And thanks for shopping at Alpha Beta!*"

"Go," Emma said. She had put her hands over her ears, maybe to shut out all of the loud squeaking supermarket cart wheels. She shuddered. Her cane slipped from one hand but I caught it.

"What if I do?"

"Then you can leave! Honest, Chase. We can all go—back where we come from."

I got off the freight elevator on the loft floor still not feeling very good. My arm, even though it was in a sling, was throbbing just from the exertion of having gone as far as the street with Chase. But I was determined to wean myself off painkillers, which along with the massive dose of antibiotics, were wrecking my stomach. And depressing my libido. I figured I could tough it out on Advil until I had the first of my skin grafts in a couple of days. I'd have scars but I wasn't going to lose fingers or, after therapy, much of the strength in my hand.

Usually there were only a couple of work lights burning in the studio, which is why the pulsating glare from a cutting torch stood out like a blue-white supernova. I smelled acetylene. The torch seemed to be burning unattended on one of two high workbenches in the studio. A thousand degrees Fahrenheit? I wasn't sure just how hot it could get but I knew those things didn't light up accidentally. I had been gone from the loft less than five minutes. Mom had assistants and part-time welders on her payroll and one or two of them she trusted most might have had a key. But the stairs were near the freight elevator; no one could have reached the studio without my knowing. There wasn't a back door, only a rusted fire escape. The rear wall of the old brewery was nearly flush with the retaining wall on the East River.

But there it was: the narrow dangerous flame of the torch glowing twenty feet away.

Easy enough to shut it off, though I could use only one hand. After that I'd try to figure out what had caused the torch to come on in the first place.

There were tall gas cylinders behind the workbench, one of them fueling the torch. I headed that way, shielding my eyes from the blinding light. I didn't smell smoke so with luck the workbench hadn't begun to smolder. I checked the location of one of the big fire extinguishers that Mom kept all over the loft.

I was near the bench when I heard the wrenching of metal, a tortured sound that damn near lifted my scalp. I saw, from the corner of my eye, a massive scrap-metal sculpture, one of Mom's jagged predatory-looking bird figures, move.

Move, as if it were about to take flight, tearing itself free of the bolts that pinned it to the concrete floor.

✦

As I went down aisle two toward the back of the Alpha Beta supermarket pushing the cart with Emma Pierce riding in it, other carts began slowly to converge, following us to the meat department.

Where there was a chilly fog around the refrigerated cases, three of them, as if someone had left open the sliding door to a cavernous walk-in locker at the rear of the butcher's shop.

The fog was part of the reason why the store didn't seem as brightly lighted as it had only a couple of minutes ago. I looked up at the fluorescent lights. They were dimming to a putrid shade of yellow, like a bad L.A. morning.

Emma also was looking up, a sense of inward seeing in the vacancy of her eyes.

"We're here," I said. "Now what?"

"They'll show you," Emma said, her voice hushed.

"Who?"

"The butchers."

And there *were* butchers present, four of them behind the cases wearing stained aprons and hair cocoons like butter-fly netting. They all were smiling, and two of them juggled a combination of knives with foot-long blades and cleavers. Making it look deft and effortless, a glittery sideshow of their profession. I didn't know what to make of them, their bizarre uncanniness.

The level of illumination in the store might have turned to a dismal twilight, but the big cases remained bright. They were packed with choice cuts of steak, mounds of ground beef or pork, rib roasts and slabs of spareribs, hawsers of sausage with each link thicker than my wrist. All of it vividly juicy, red and pink and stomach-turning. At least to me. But I'd always had to deal with a touchy stomach.

"All right," I said. "Here I am. Now why am I here?"

The juggling butchers concluded their act and put down the cutlery. All four, still smiling through the puffs of fog from within the freight-car-size freezer locker behind them, turned with the synchronized panache of a blue-ribbon barbershop quartet, bowing in turn to the one case that wasn't lighted.

That one, as I looked blinking through the freezing fog, appeared to be empty.

I passed the back of a hand across my forehead. My eyebrows felt brittle from frost. I had been trembling before; now I was shaking violently. I kept my eyes on the large case in which I saw nothing.

A spark appeared in the slanted glass, a starry flaw that became a brilliant zigzag of lightning. It hurt my eyes and I looked away.

Emma gave me a little push with both hands.

"Go closer," she said.

But I was already edging away from her and the cart, my head lowered, my face averted because I was afraid of another of those telltale, signature bolts of lightning on the glass.

Lights flickered on inside the case as I leaned toward the glass, my hands spread on it for support.

I looked upon the centerpiece, the full horror of what had

been prepared for me, splattering the glass with my vomit but still seeing, *seeing*: and realizing then what was happening, or about to happen, six blocks away in Stella Moritz's loft.

I couldn't get to the cylinders of gas or the torch to turn it off—that gawky angular bird my mother had crafted from painted scrap metal and what looked like chain mail leaped into my path, jagged wings scything. They missed me by less than a foot as I scrambled away.

Even as the rational mind tries to reject what it knows to be impossible (like a coronal of thorny vine changing into a six-foot rattlesnake with the speed of a magician shaking a dove from a handkerchief), the atavistic brain reacts only to what the eyes take in. I was being attacked by a suddenly animated piece of sculpture, as if the flat one-eyed peckerish head had a brain and reason to resent me to go with its terrifying screeches of ripped sheet metal. My only impulse was to get the hell away and sort out the illogic later. Much later.

But there was a companion bird sculpture, as if Mom had had so much fun and artistic satisfaction building the first one.

Occupied by the menace confronting me, I hadn't been aware of the other pulling up bolts as well. I saw it only as a flighty shadow coming between me and the freight elevator, landing on spindly bird legs with a clatter, spreading flash chrome wings to cut off my only escape route.

By then I had backed into the other workbench and was circling it, keeping the bench between me and the orange-hued bird stalking me.

Realistic but totally unreal. The absolute absurdity of the situation may have appealed to me in a subliminal way. I'd once thought in the depths of my theological convulsions I had seen an angel sitting at the foot of my bed sadly shaking its head at me. I could have used an angel now. But the fight-or-flight instinct had completely taken over, putting my sanity on the shelf. I had a quick look at what was available for fighting back in the collection of neatly stored hand tools at the back of the bench.

An eight-pound hammer with two feet of hickory handle seemed to be my best bet. What could be assembled by bolt and solder could also be disassembled, I reasoned, panicky though I was.

Unfortunately I had only one hand and arm to work with. Swinging an eight-pound hammer could quickly become tiring if you weren't used to it.

I scrambled again holding on to the hammer as a huge wing slashed down, cutting a groove in hard maple, a worktop slab five inches thick.

Back-pedaling, I blindsided an eight-foot wooden stepladder and fell with it to the floor. I had a leg hooked inside two steps of the heavy ladder and couldn't jerk it free.

Both birds came slowly after me, their stupid dangerous heads nodding.

If only Stella Moritz had taken up painting instead.

∕

The hacked body of Adam, looking cloistral inside misted glass, had been laid out autopsy-fashion for me to see and regret. All limbs in place but his naked body unjointed like a chicken cut up for frying.

Apart from the vivid horror of seeing him like that I felt a floating disorientation, my head lolling uncontrollably. I couldn't touch the floor with my feet. But I didn't fall. Spectators, that funereal bunch of shoppers, had pressed closer. Two pairs of hands reached out to keep me upright.

"See what you done?" Emma Pierce cried. "This's all your fault, Chase!"

Crow had told her to say that, I was sure. But of course, I knew it was true. My fault, and I sobbed guiltily, accepting the judgment. Time had jolted forward, hours had disappeared from my allotted span and Adam had been neatly butchered while I was letting little Emma distract me outside the marketplace.

No tears had come to my eyes. I stopped sobbing. Then, weirdly and soullessly, I began to laugh, a laugh that echoed as a curse on my fate and my futile attempts to escape it.

My head stopped hanging so uselessly. I could almost think straight again, and I began to react against the press of softly groaning mourners, the hands tugging at my parka. I saw only vague shapes in the mist, but closer the hands that held me so insistently looked desiccated, nearly skeletal: bones showed through jerky-dried flesh. I flailed at the hands with my own and stumbled away from the butcher's corner of the store, knocking over the cart Emma had been riding in.

Her little body imploded into dust within her clothes. Her jaunty blue tam flew away like a bird as her skull separated from neck bones and rolled on the floor.

I jumped over the toppled cart, shoving bodies from my path, and ran up the aisle toward what I thought must be daylight coming through the windows that faced the street. I caromed off another figure motionless behind a cart and he fell with a long-dead grin to the floor. I couldn't avoid stepping on him. His caving-in chest made a whooshing sound and I recoiled from a gust of grave air, retching again. My feet crossed, which almost never happened no matter what game I was in, and I fell backward against shelves of cooking oil. Gallons of the stuff also fell and split open, greasing me and the aisle around me.

Then I slipped and slid trying to run again, and took out a display pyramid of tomato sauce in glass bottles. Half of them fell in bomb bursts of shards and mucky sauce.

By the time I reached the street, having pried apart doors that refused to slide open for me, I looked like pizza-to-go.

Outside the sky was still blue and cloudless. The sidewalk was filled with strollers. None of them were stopping at the Alpha Beta, though. Because the windows behind me were blank, smeared with bar soap or paint, and the sign over the doors was missing. A hand-lettered sign on one door said that the supermarket had relocated two blocks farther east on Broadway.

Maybe I should have known that. But I was new to the neighborhood.

This one. But not Crow Tillman's neighborhood. And that's what made me scream in frustration as I ran back to Stella Moritz's loft.

I drew stares and I saw frightened faces, but they all got out of my way fast. No one wanted to try to stop a crazed woman with what might have been blood on her hands and clothing. Six blocks to run, and never a cop around when you needed one. If there had been, I guess they only would have slowed me down.

When I got to the former brewery the elevator wasn't there. I didn't think I had time to wait for it to come down. There was a din from the loft. No way to describe it. Adam yelling. Another shock to my system. I'd half convinced myself I would find him dead. I paused for only a few seconds to catch my breath, then I sprinted up the badly-lit iron stairs, making a racket of my own.

The loft quieted down a few seconds before I kicked open the sticking door to the studio and stumbled in, winded again.

"Adam!"

He was standing at one end of a large workbench, a welder's helmet tipped up on his head. He turned toward me, extinguished the hissing torch in his gloved hand. He leaned against the bench and breathed through his mouth. Near him were two piles of scrap metal. I recognized a wing from one of Stella Moritz's birds.

There was a burnt, metallic odor in the air, a floating haze.

He laid the torch on the bench. Dropped the welder's glove. His hand was shaking.

"They came after me," he said.

"What?"

"Mom's birds."

"They did what?"

"You should have seen them."

"You don't know what *I* saw."

"Are you hurt, Chase?"

"What?" I said again, and looked myself over as I walked slowly and sloppily toward him. "No, it's just oil and tomato sauce."

Behind me I heard the elevator whine and start down with the usual jolting two-foot drop. I more or less collapsed against the workbench beside Adam.

"Oil and tomato sauce," he said.

"It's real. The experience at the market was phantasmagorical."

"So was this," he said, gesturing at the still-hot piles of metal.

"Your mother taught you how to use a welding torch?"

"Cutting torch."

"We're putting a stop to all this," I said. "I'm not having any more of it."

"Okay. How?"

"There's only one way. I have to go to the Netherworld and kill Crow Tillman."

"Kill a dead man."

"There's dead, and there's not so dead."

"You did tell me that. Okay. I'm all for it. I'll back you up all the way."

"I know you would, sweet angel, but you're not going."

"I know the way."

"Do you know the way back?"

"Do you?"

We didn't say anything for a couple of minutes.

"So you've got a plan?" Adam said.

"Did I say that? But I'll get a plan."

"Okay," he said doubtfully.

We listened to the elevator rising toward the loft.

"Oh-oh," I said. "No time to clean up. What are you—"

"Let me do the talking."

"I wouldn't want to be you right now," I said. "Actually I don't want to be me, either. Is there room to hide under this workbench?"

"Be brave. It's like living near Mount Rushmore. After a while you don't even notice."

The elevator stopped and the gate was raised by a uniformed chauffeur. Adam's mother materialized from behind a stack of six matched pieces of luggage and a wardrobe trunk and walked off towing a carry-on.

"You're back!" Adam called cheerfully.

Stella Moritz was a tall, you might say stately, woman with cropped silver-and-black hair, round dark eyes in a small head, and an aggressively squared jaw. She had one of those small taut mouths that were not given to smiling. She looked around, stopped, sniffed the air, shot a look at Adam.

I made an attempt to soften what was shaping up as a tense homecoming by walking toward her with a little self-effacing hand gesture. Not exactly my style, but. Some bits of metal crunched beneath my sneakers. At closer range I saw that her face had the slightly wizened appearance of a granny apple left too long on a windowsill. Her tanned skin was a dark ochre shade.

"Hi, I'm Chase," I said.

She checked me out. I checked myself out and laughed, too girlishly.

"I don't always look like this."

She left me dangling for several seconds.

"Oh," she said finally. "Good." Maybe if I'd had time to buy flowers? She dismissed me, giving all of her attention to Adam. "What the hell happened to my studio? And just what have you done to my birds?"

"Since the snake bit me on the subway I've had nightmares. I dreamed the birds were attacking me. Finally I couldn't stand it anymore." Adam looked around at the wreckage with an apologetic shrug. "I hope they weren't all that valuable."

"Today's market, I'd say about a hundred twenty-five thousand apiece. We'll discuss. After we have you settled in with a good psychoanalyst."

"Chase and I are going to be married," Adam said, searching for something favorable to report.

"Don't invite me," Stella Moritz said, towing her little case around me on her way to the living quarters.

I had said fewer than ten words to her, but I stood there frozen in place, feeling humiliated. Wondering if there ever would be a way of explaining myself to her.

Adam walked over to me and put his good arm around my shoulders.

"Nightmares," he said. "That didn't sound too glib, did it?"

"I'll help you clean up," I said. "Then we have to get out of here. We must, Adam."

"Is this a woman-thing?"

"You shouldn't have to ask."

Adam
January 13–15.

You know how she is," Dory said to me. "A total fussbudget when it comes to her tools and her workplace. Every item on her benches in precise order. The floor swept clean at least twice a day. Woe to those around her if a stray sliver of metal or a peanut-size piece of granite disturbs her concentration. Tell me the truth. You did it on purpose, didn't you? You were acting out, like neither of us could ever afford to do because her scorn withers. It withers the hearts of impressionable children. But this was payback time. You had an orgasmic release from a lifetime of tension and frustration. A Freudian conniption. The snake figures into it somehow."

"Wasn't like that at all," I said.

Dory was peeling an orange with her teeth.

"I'd love to have seen it."

"The snake?"

"The scene of epic destruction." She broke the orange into quarters and handed me one.

Chase and I had been staying with Dory while we made wedding plans. Chase had gone shopping and was taking a nap. We were going to be married in two days' time. Dory as maid of honor, Sergei Olanovsky as best man at his house on the lower Housatonic. I had borrowed two thousand dollars from Dory, for Chase's trousseau and for setting up housekeeping until my arm was healed and I could go back to being a campus cop and trying to figure out something better to do with myself. Chase had made a phone call and was offered a position in the math department at Southern Connecticut State University in New Haven while she worked on the book she said she wanted to write.

"I was a somnambulist possessed by a nightmare. Smashing and torching those birds cured me. Should I invite Mom anyway?"

"Let me talk to her. She can be coaxed, if you go about it the right way. What's this with Chase and her eyelids? Sounds neurotic and self-willed to me. Although I appreciate the fact that sometimes you just have to shut your eyes and keep the world away."

"Right," I said.

"Would it be safe to make reservations at Patsy's tonight?"

"Neither of us makes scenes in public," I said. I finished the last segment of orange Dory had given me and went looking for Chase. If she was still sleeping, fine. I'd just sit in a corner of the Ethan Allen bedroom and watch her on the four-poster, comforter tucked around her. Listen to her breathe through slightly parted lips.

But she was awake. She sat in the west window bay with arms folded, bare feet tucked under her, head down toward one shoulder like a lazy swan. From the window there was a clear view of the Hudson River, choppy in the wind. The sun came and went brilliantly on a partly cloudy day. Her eyes opened and narrowed according to the rhythm of the sunlight flooding the glass.

"One third of a mile," she said, seeing my reflection in the glass when I walked in. "He was walking, as he told us later, away from the blast site at what anyone would believe was a safe distance: 586.67 yards, or 536.22 meters. Rounded off. Approximately the length of six football fields. It was 1:45 in the afternoon on the twenty-sixth of July. Without taking into account his exact height, the length of his stride, the air temperature and humidity at that hour, wind speed and direction, the gradient where he was walking, the possibility of a small swarm of insects in the air between him and the blast site that could account for a slight deflection, the odds that a piece of rock weighing about two ounces and in a totally random trajectory, traveling at, say, 900 f.p.s., the speed of a bullet leaving the muzzle of a 1911-model Colt .45 automatic, impacting the fourth cervical vertebra and all but destroying it along with a millimeter of spinal cord, are 2.13 billion to one."

"Is this about Jimmy?" I said, sitting on the window seat beside her.

"I really miss him today."

"A fragment of rock endowed with malevolent intent," I said. "We know Crow Tillman can influence events from where he is. Like a 'roid-rage poltergeist."

"One of the more bizarre aspects of quantum mechanics. Which a lot of physicists hate because it's unobservable. Lewis Little would call what Crow does 'vitalistic psychokinesis.' In other words, bullshit. Conceptually I don't believe quantum theory either. I just live it."

She snuggled closer to me.

"Do you have a plan yet?" I said.

"No."

"I've been thinking. Crow's not all that smart. I suppose animating a pair of sheet-metal birds struck him as a great idea. But all I had to do was knock their skinny bird legs out from under them with the hammer and they were helpless. *Pow-pow.*"

Chase kissed my cheek, then put the tip of her tongue in my ear. An erotic treat she employed sparingly but always to good effect. Sensational might be a better word.

"That's for keeping your wits about you."

"He can't scare us. Anyway, how pissed is Crow going to be when he finds out we're getting married?"

"I'm sure he knows already."

"Might as well invite him to the wedding, then."

Chase turned my head gently to purse her lips against my other ear. Her silence then seemed deep and filled with hazard.

"No need," she said at last. "He'll show up. Or *something* will."

The reality of what we faced was a racing shadow, clouding ardor until blood heat dissolved it. As blood and true love always did, in mundane reality or timeless epic myth.

"Chase, is there any way to get to Tillman—I don't know, take him by surprise, drive a stake through his heart?"

"That's vampires," she said with a slight forgiving smile. "Crow is—"

"Yeah, undead."

"I can't keep him out of my head. It's like trying to flush a rat from an attic. All I can do to keep him away from my soul during Spaz. *That* he will never have."

I had the use of both my hands again, although the left was still swollen and I could barely crook my fingers without a lot of pain. I began to undress her on the window seat, warmed and fearless in dappled afternoon sun. Pop of electricity as I pulled Chase's cableknit sweater off over her burnished honey-gold head, an agreeable shock to both of us.

"But there won't be anything left for our wedding night," Chase protested demurely.

"I've been reading this book," I said. "A secret sex diary kept in Victorian times. Would you believe, those buttoned-up Vics liked doing the same things we do? There are some informative woodcuts."

"You've been reading a book."

Chase slowly unbuttoned her shirt with a sigh I took to be contentment.

"I'm looking forward to what you learned in chapter two," she said.

Her heart in her eyes, mine alone to see.

(After making love: the sensual happiness of a shower like steady warm rain.)

For a while it is possible to believe we are like any other about-to-be-wed couple, thinking of nothing but the mercies of each other, without a lingering curse on their periphery.

Dory was working at home on a Friday, studying layouts for an upcoming issue of *Charisma*, looking at digitals of a photo shoot in some distant exotic place, keeping an eye on a popular afternoon talk show that featured one of those cultural super-organisms who have the density of mind and lack of wit of a coffee can full of lug nuts.

Dory looked away from her sixty-inch LCD screen and took a pencil from between her teeth.

"Is it Christmas or Easter Island that has the stupendously big heads?

"Congress, I think. Have you called Mom?"

"She's not picking up. I ordered the flowers from a shop I know in Westport."

"Thanks, Dory."

"Shall I keep trying Mom? I mean, do you really want her there?"

"Chase does," I said.

On Saturday afternoon, the day before our wedding, Sergei Olanovsky invited us to tour his facility at the Frohlinger Research Institute.

When we got there half a dozen chimps were socializing or exercising in their play area. Lab assistants were uncrating a couple of hyperbaric chambers. Sergei was ecstatic.

"The funding finally was approved," he said. "Two years we have waited."

"What are they for?" I said.

"For saturating body and brain tissue with oxygen during resuscitation attempts. Moving us closer to the day, perhaps, when we will successfully revive human victims who are clinically dead due to a variety of causes: smoke inhalation, carbon monoxide poisoning, loss of blood—"

"Or drowning," Chase said.

Sergei beamed. "Your recovery, from what I've been able to learn, is rare and remarkable. I'm looking forward to talking to you about it. Not on this happy occasion, of course. For later, at your discretion and convenience."

"I wouldn't be able to tell you very much. They took me by helicopter to Atlanta. Emory University Hospital. Why don't you try accessing their records, Dr. Olanovsky? Talk to the doctors who were on my case."

"I will. Thank you very much for the information." Sergei embraced us both. "What a lovely bride! Such a beautiful couple! I am so happy for both of you. I must warn, I always cry at weddings. The drunker I get, the more I cry."

*

The ceremony took about five minutes, on the glassed-in terrace of Sergei's house overlooking a wide bend in the floe-laden river, which was almost a mile across. I wore my best and only blue suit. Chase carried a nosegay of forget-me-nots and other small hothouse flowers. She wore a long pale blue skirt and a navy embroidered bolero jacket. We exchanged simple gold rings.

I paid the minister, who was a stranger to everybody, we posed for photographs, and Sergei enthusiastically uncorked the Dom Perignon, of a vintage he claimed was the finest in thirty years. His treat.

Chase and I had a flute apiece. Sergei tripled our intake in only a few minutes. He put some hectic Russian folk music on his Bose system. Like he'd promised, he got drunk and cried a lot and kissed all of us often.

Dory had come up on the train and was spending the night at the house of one of her chums, whom she had roomed with at Wellesley. Chase and I drove her down to Westport in my drafty Datsun. We dropped her on one of those little lanes between Imperial and another river, the Saugatuck. Her friend gave us directions for finding the Turnpike southbound.

Married and alone at last. We smiled at each other as I drove, the kind of lavish smiles newlyweds have for each other, but with that little degree of uncertainty to them. *Am I sure I wanted to do this?*

"Well."

"Well."

I held her gloved hand, not taking my eye off the road as it made a wide bend, the river coming into view again, along with the old narrow swing bridge that crossed it.

"Did it bother you that my mother wasn't there?" I said.

"A little, I think. Were you hurt, Adam?"

"I don't know yet. As a kid I learned to bury my filial resentments instantly, like a hound with a fresh soup bone. Bury them deep in some out-of-the-way place in the psyche."

"Oh. That's bad. Sooner or later those old bones have to be dug up, otherwise you're miserable for all of your adult life. Why not just say you were hurt because she was a no-show, get it out and over with. I think your mom will always regret that she didn't come."

"Or not. Okay. I was . . . hurt. It hurts. There. Said and done."

I looked at Chase. Her eyes had closed. She had the tense expression I'd seen before, when EBS occurred. I squeezed her hand.

"Chase?"

She let out her breath and relaxed. "I guess the timing could've been worse." She laid her head back on the seat. I drove onto the river bridge, a span of less than a hundred yards here, with Long Island Sound not half a mile to the south, aglow in late afternoon sunbreak through high scudding clouds. There was moderate traffic on those two lanes across the Saugatuck. I automatically registered the approach of a ten-ton truck from the other side. The bridge rumbled, and my Datsun, which could have used new shocks, bounced a little, pulling left.

"Now don't you feel better?" Chase said.

Then she sat bolt upright, eyes still sealed, with a look of terror.

"Adam!"

We had been married for only a couple of hours. So little time. Now all we had was about to be taken away from us.

He appeared, in jeans and denim jacket and cocky straw hat, as if he were just strolling down the center of the bridge, out for an afternoon's walk. But the hat he wore was fully aflame, and there was a dark pit of congealed blood and brain on the left side of his head, where half the ear was missing.

Crow Tillman turned and grinned at us as I drove through him and into the opposite lane in front of the oncoming truck. I hit the brake but was unable to control the steering.

"Adam, what's HAPPENING?" Chase screamed.

I saw the face of the truck driver as he was turning his wheel hard left to miss the Datsun. But there was no room on that bridge for such maneuvers.

From the look on his face it crossed my mind that he also had seen the apparition two seconds ago.

The bridge railings were steel, but old, possibly corroded. But they might have withstood the impact of the small sedan—if the high square body of the truck hadn't come around, wheels leaving the bridge pavement on the other side, lifting, then smashing down on the back end of the Datsun, adding a lot of weight to our sideways momentum.

The railing and fence snapped and flattened. The Datsun lurched over the side of the bridge, hung there momentarily as I tried to free myself from my seat belt, then rolled heavily off and down to the high-tide river as Chase screamed again.

There is always a chance of escaping from a submerged vehicle under some conditions and if the luck factor is there. But it wasn't working out for us as the hood of the Datsun twisted and came loose on impact and smashed open the windshield. Locked into our seat harnesses, we were instantly engulfed in near-freezing water. The Datsun sank quickly, side-down.

Blind and drowning, Chase clawed at me, numbly pleading with her hands for help.

I couldn't move. I couldn't help her. I could only look at her. Until I didn't see her anymore.

Netherworld

Tap, tap.

THE CAMERA'S EYE

At a depth of twenty feet in the Saugatuck River there is light, but not much light, from the sky on a waning winter afternoon.

PUSHING SLOWLY DOWN, THE CAMERA FINDS:

The Datsun, a water-filled coffin, lying on its side.

If the man and woman trapped in the car could see to the surface of the river, and beyond, they would make out the spidery superstructure of the bridge from which the car has plummeted. They would have no trouble identifying the winking light bars of rescue vehicles on the bridge.

Although their eyes are open, they see none of this. They see only each other's slightly engorged, bluish faces.

Tap, tap.

And now there are boats, three of them, from a nearby marina, propellers churning the water to keep the boats hovering above the indistinct shape of the car at full tide.

IN THE CAR—A CLOSE TWO SHOT

The lovers reach out to each other.

Tap, tap, tap.

Someone's there.

Chase, hanging in her seat harness at a cramped diagonal to the intact window on her side of the car, twists her head to have a look.

REVERSE ANGLE

Outside the water has brightened, as if a newly risen nether sun shines fully down upon them. The water is no longer near to freezing. It feels just right—refreshing as a tepid bath after a long sultry summer's day.

CHASE'S POV*

She sees outside her window a floating boy. Ten or eleven years old. Just floating, facedown, baggy overalls, eyeing them curiously.

He taps again on the window, almost playfully.

Adam, I think he wants us to go with him.

Do you know him?

No. But he looks all right. No harm in him is what I mean.

Well. We shouldn't stay here. Can you roll down your window?

I think so.

Let's go then.

POV—THE SUNKEN CAR

Chase does roll down the window without difficulty. The floating boy, who is wearing only overalls, no shirt, no shoes, approves of this and gestures for the two of them to follow. He turns, then sprints away with a flick of his pale feet easy as a fish to a shallow place of cattails and gently wavering reeds. A good place for fish to feed. But, curiously, there are none.

---

* Point of view

CLOSEUP—CHASE'S ENTRANCED EXPRESSION

PUSH IN TO THE BOY

Where he turns to wait with lazy motions of his hands the river has shaded from murky gray to clear blue and is softly alight, star-surfaced, shot through with shimmering beams adagio in this blue element.

All of the pockets of the boy's overalls are packed and lumpy with horseshoes and smooth stones. Yet he has no problem maintaining his vertical position in the current, feet dangling well above the river bottom.

(He is a drowned boy. Somehow Chase knows this. But she feels no astonishment, sadness, or terror in knowing. Because they all are drowned here, not where life has ended, but where it will resume. On different terms. Her face also is alight, with eagerness. She looks at Adam, but he doesn't understand yet.)

ON CHASE AND ADAM

Together they slip out of their seat harnesses and rise nakedly, almost without effort, upward through the window space, swim side by side from deeper grimmer waters to the boy in the shallows. When Chase looks back there is no sign of the wrecked Datsun. That part of the river already lies beyond her field of vision. If she wanted to think purposefully of anything right now she would look only to what surely lies ahead.

But she is content to swim somewhat dreamily beside her lover, rolling over a time or two, kicking leisurely.

A POOL IN A SHADOWY NOON GLADE—SUMMER—DAY

The Drowned Boy, as we will know him, climbs out of the pool to a low bank hung with deep green ferns and cooled by a sunscreen of weeping willows. When Chase's head breaks the surface of the eddy pool he reaches down for her.

Soon they are all seated or stretched out on the gently sloping embankment. Adam's expression is stunned as he looks down at his body, nude in sunflash, and at Chase, equally nude. The Drowned Boy hugs his knees in the cutoff raggedy overalls and smiles slightly to himself, neither looking at them nor wanting to make anything of their sprawled pale bodies.

There's clothes for yall in the truck, he says. He leans forward to spit at his reflection on the surface of the pool.

Chase is the first to rise. She gives her head a shake and her hair is instantly dry. She puts down a comforting hand to Adam. Knowing what he is going through right now. He looks up at her touch, blinking, unable to speak. But the question is in his eyes.

Yes, Chase says. This is partly how it was for me the first time. Others who pulled me from the river. There is always a river, a body of water.

She turns to the Drowned Boy.

Where is the truck?

He turns his head. Yonder on the road.

Thank you. And thanks for—

Well it wa'n't nothin much, he says with a bashful head shake. I fetch folks all the time. It's somethin a do, you know.

I expect that's true. Because nothing ever happens here, does it?

Just square-dancin. Ever'body likes to dance.

How long have you been here?

CLOSE ON THE DROWNED BOY

He shrugs, smiles unknowingly. If he had any idea, it still wouldn't matter to him.

CHASE KNEELS BESIDE ADAM

Sweet angel, come with me.

ON THE ROAD BEYOND THE GLADE AND PARALLEL TO THE RIVER

There is a Silverado pickup truck, streaks of red clay along the body as if it has been driven hard on wet unpaved back roads. It looks just like it did the last time Chase saw it, by the lights of helicopters at the campground in the Chattahoochee National Forest.

She stops for a few moments, staring at the truck, her grip tightening on Adam's hand.

What is it, Chase?

Nothing. *Everything.* Now I know exactly where I am.

Who is that man?

I don't know.

The man is of late middle-age, heavyset, with a sun-coarsened face and hooded blue eyes out of sync with each other. He leans in full sun against a front fender of the silver pickup with the roof rack of swamp lights and the heavy-duty bumper and radiator guard. His arms are loosely folded. He has the attitude of someone who spends a lot of time just waiting. He's wearing a black suit on a hot day and a white shirt with a high collar. Buttoned. There's an old beat-up salt-streaked gray fedora pushed back on his head, riding a shock of black hair shot through with silver. His expression is uncomplainingly benign. An old workhorse, no expectations, no demands.

CHASE AND ADAM RESUME THEIR APPROACH TO THE TRUCK

I thought he might be—

No. Neither kith nor kin of the Curdy brothers. Nor of Talis Lawhorn. Crow Tillman, well, I can't be sure.

The man at the truck, hearing her, straightens and unfolds his arms.

No, ma'am. Ain't no kin a Crow Tillman. I was long 'fore his time.

Chase feels Adam shudder through the hand she clasps. The shudders continue as he looks around.

That's all right, she says calmingly.

255

This place—it's like looking at one of those antique post-cards. A little too colorful. Three-dimensional, but still—something's missing.

Life itself, Adam.

That's it. Yes. The busyness of life, a dimension of sound, of weather. It's hot, but we're not sweating. The sky is clear and blue, but no birds, no birds. Or animals, or insects. It's too still here. I hate it!

CLOSE ON ADAM

He struggles to come to terms with the fact of his dying.

TRACKING CHASE

She leaves Adam, walks to the truck and the waiting man, who respectfully removes his old fedora.

Hot here in the daytime, Chase says.

It be hot ever' day, yes ma'am. Nights is cooler. The moon is always full.

The man holds his head at a wry angle. Welcome, he says. Name's Walter Higgins.

I'm Chase. My husband is Adam.

The wall-eyed man studies Adam in the road.

Don't know as how he's expected.

No?

But I don't have no say in such matters.

You brought us clothes, Mr. Higgins?

Just you. Reckon there's some to spare for your husband. You look to be close to the same size. I'll just fetch them garments outen the truck and hope they be to your liken.

Crow Tillman's truck, isn't it?

Yes, ma'am. He said it would be bygones with you.

No. Not yet. Not by a damn sight.

Chase has her own look around the partly wooded countryside drowsing in the sun, silently naming the churches of the steeples she sees until Walter Higgins has fetched her a pair of running shorts, jeans, a Nike T-shirt, and a short-sleeved pale yellow blouse. The shoes are sturdy Doc Martens, like those she began wearing at age thirteen. There's also a pair of neoprene shower clogs.

Walter Higgins folds his arms and looks off, squinting his wayward eye. Adam joins Chase and they split the clothing.

Looks like I wasn't expected, he says. (Something else to puzzle over with dread and uncertainty.) Does this mean I might be going back?

I don't know, sweet angel.

Without you, no way.

Let's get dressed.

She hands the T-shirt, running shorts and clogs to Adam, knowing that the jeans and shoes won't fit him.

The Drowned Boy saunters their way from the glade, if anyone with twenty-five pounds of stones and horseshoes in his pockets could be said to saunter. He is still sopping wet.

Gee-ho-se-phat! he says, admiring the huge silver truck. Don't it look like a chariot from a storybook.

You ought to get out of those wet overalls, Adam says.

Naw. Just have to go on a-wearin 'em.

Why?

Adam.

That's right, that's right, Walter Higgins says as he nods his awkwardly hanging head. Just have to go on a-wearin 'em. Walter unbuttons his high shirt collar. His head falls aslant at an even steeper angle.

Like I wear this, he says.

Beneath the now-open collar are the remains of a hanging rope.

Otherwise I'd've cut this here rope off long ago. Cain't do that, leastwise till I go before the Committee.

Aware of Adam's perplexity, Walter further volunteers: I shot my woman for lyin with 'nother man. Reckon I should have just accepted my mortal judgment at the time, and moved on.

Will you ever move on from the Netherworld? Adam says, avoiding another scolding look from Chase.

That would be up to the Committee, son.

How big is the Netherworld? Is this all there is?

No, sir. The Netherworld, reckon she's as big as need be to hold ever'body's grief and folly and shame. This here part of it is all I know about. Few miles thataway, few more miles over there. 'Bout what I was used to 'fore I met the hangin rope.

Me too, the Drowned Boy says. He pulls a stone twice the size of his fist from one of the breast pockets of the overalls.

Water slides in rivulets down his face from his drenched flattened cowlick. He grins proudly.

Couldn't take Pa's beatin's no more, he says. He puts the stone back. So I jumped down the well. Reckon I was there a couple months 'fore they noticed the water tastin funny.

Looking at Chase, he says, What did *you* do?

Chase and Adam exchange looks.

CLOSE ON CHASE

There is a look of grim resolve in her eyes as she pulls on her jeans.

I haven't done it yet, she says.

HIGH ANGLE (AERIAL)—THE PICKUP TRUCK—DAY

Walter Higgins drives, drives poorly, as if the act of steering baffles him. The truck, except for the sounds the tires make on gravel, is utterly quiet.

CAMERA PUSHES DOWN AND TRACKS THE SILVERADO

Chase and Adam are in the front seat of the quad cab with Walter Higgins. The Drowned Boy rides in the bed of the truck, faceup in the sun, smiling, his eyes closed. He is still soaking wet.

It's just the same, Chase tells Adam in a hushed voice.

What is?

The cab of Crow's truck. His little booklet of porn photos of some of his conquests dangling from the mirror post—

Surely do apologize for that, Walter says. He is red of face. But the truck, she ain't mine to make no changes.

The Star quilt we're sitting on, Chase says. The smell of it. You couldn't wash out all the stink if you tried. The tobacco he smoked. The stale beer. Who knows whatall. That wormy dog! It gripes me no end. How could Mama stand that man for long?

Adam says, This truck is running on empty. I can't hear the engine.

It just runs because it's got someplace to go, Walter Higgins says. That's all there is to it.

Chase looks around the cab of the Silverado, frowning.

One thing is different. There was a hunting knife on the dashboard. It's gone. Do you know where that knife is, Mr. Higgins?

Believe I saw him take it out a here before he bid me and the boy to fetch you.

Chase, Adam says.

Yes.

He's taking us to Crow Tillman.

Yes.

Why?

Because it's what we've always wanted. Crow and me. From the night he shot himself. It's taken me a long time to understand that it has to happen. And how, and where.

At twenty miles an hour in the truck they slowly overtake a man, a woman, and three children walking beside the road.

There's Soames, Walter Higgins says of the man.

THE SOAMES FAMILY

Walking single file. The father is barefoot, wearing only a sagging pair of long johns. His throat looks freshly cut, ear to ear. The woman behind him wears burnt tatters. Her hair is ashes. Most of her skin area is the purplish red shade of third-degree burns. The children, looking up as the truck passes them, are in various states of ambulatory char.

Soames, he was lyin drunk in the barn loft when the house lit up at Christmastime, his family snug in their beds.

Where are they going? Chase says.

Same place as you. To the dancin.

When will it start? The dancing?

Right at dark, when the full moon's riz. That'd be tonight. And ever' night hereafter, of course.

CLOSE ON OUR THREESOME IN THE TRUCK CAB

There's a full moon every night? Adam says.

Sun in the mornin, moon at night. Never changes. Well—almost never. Except when the Tempests come. But they is few and far between. Only seen two of 'em myself.

You mean a storm?

Walter Higgins squints his wayward eye.

A black, howlin storm. Made blacker by lumps a coal and worse come a rainin down on those that cain't find shelter till it's done passed. The Tempest comes for *souls*. The most terrible fate a soul can call down upon itself. You ain't never seen nothin like it. You ain't wantin to.

What I've seen, Adam says, is a black dog.

To Chase Walter Higgins says, Reckon you're a knowin where this road leads, ain't ye missy?

Yes, Chase says, a pall of sadness in her eyes.

There be time to stop a spell at your home place if it would please you.

Is my mother there?

No'm. The Committee done passed her on almost as soon as she lighted here. Passed her on to her fair and just reward.

What Committee? Adam says.

Them souls that has earned the right to judge other souls.

The Committee sounds like the Tempest to me, Adam says.

No sir! The Tempest stands alone. It be the final, terrible Judgment.

I want to move on to the Campground, Chase says to Walter Higgins. Let's have it over with.

Yes'm. Well, we'uns is almost there.

I don't see how that could be, Mr. Higgins. The Campground is almost fifty miles from my home.

It's comin up just over the next rise. And it'll be dark real soon now. Any minute. You can see the moon now, cain't you, creepin above the ridgeline?

CAMPGROUND—THE CHATTAHOOCHEE NATIONAL
FOREST—NIGHT

HOLD ON A FULL YELLOW-ORANGE MOON

Looking huge, shining mistily over the forested Blue Ridge
and, more distant, the mighty Appalachians.

We're hearing fiddles and guitars as—

CAMERA PUSHES DOWN TO THE SILVERADO

Which glides into the Campground almost as if the wheels
aren't touching the dense needlepack beneath tall loblollies
that fence in the open space and a scattering of plank picnic tables with benches.

At the edge of the Campground is a floor of pine boards
worn smooth and even by who knows how many dancing feet
over what span of time in a timeless place. There is also a gaze-
bolike bandstand where five musicians (two fiddles, a standing
bass, two guitars) are tuning up for the square dance. Those
dancers who stand patiently on all four sides of the floor waiting for the Caller's invitation have only the moon for illumination. They are motley dressed, some in long-out-of-fashion
corpse clothes. Beyond them, in the gorge below, the tumbling
falls throw off a cold silver light.

Chase gets out of the truck with Adam and after a few moments she points wordlessly to the rustic footbridge that
crosses the gorge. He nods and holds her close. No warmth to

share in either of their bodies. No heartbeats. Still they want to hold, and be held.

Is he there? Adam says. With the dancers?

I don't think so.

Who are those people? The ones sitting around the table over there.

The Drowned Boy jumps down from the bed of the pickup truck.

Them's the Committee.

That's right, that's right, Walter Higgins says, his low-slung head wagging loosely on his snapped neck.

THE COMMITTEE

Four men, two women. They sit at the table next to the piled stone barbecue Pit, a massive thing twice a man's height and filled with darkness. Not a lick of flame to be seen.

From the Pit, or perhaps a secret place beyond it, comes the wail of an infant.

CLOSE ON CHASE

Shock and fear.

Music. The square dance has begun.

Choose yer partners and do-see-do.

Chase turns to Adam, gasping.

QUICK CUTS TO THE DANCERS

AND BACK TO CHASE AND ADAM

It can't be! *No!*

What is it, Chase? Adam says, then looks around as the child cries again. Chase reacts by grabbing her belly, as if she's suddenly in terrible pain.

There can't be any babies *here!*

Behind them the Drowned Boy shakes his head mournfully.

'Cause babies can't be borned here.

Walter Higgins looks thoughtfully at Chase, takes off his old fedora and crushes it against his chest.

But sometimes . . . they do come, missy.

Chase looks at him in astonishment and grief.

But I—it was all arranged! I only saw him once. Then they took him away! To a good home, a *deserving* mother. He can't *be* here, don't you all understand?

First ye allemande left, then ye allemande right . . . now ye grab your honeys and hold em tight!

Chase, what are you talking about? Adam says.

Crow I'm talking about! But no. He couldn't have. He *wouldn't.* Not even Crow Tillman has that much evil in him!

She breaks away from Adam and runs across the campground toward the massive Pit, screaming Crow's name.

A tall man rises quickly from the picnic table and steps in Chase's path. He wears homespun, suspenders, a stovepipe hat. His beard full blown, patriarchal.

Missy, a word with ye.

The frightened cry of the child grows louder as Chase comes to a stop and stares up at the man, then looks at the other faces of the members of the Committee.

WHERE IS HE? Distraught, furious.

In his place, a woman says. Something in her gaze has a calming effect. She holds Chase's eyes until Chase is no longer trembling from outrage. Then the woman nods. Her wrinkled hands have been folded on the table in front of her. Now she lifts them, revealing a hunting knife with a partially serrated edge.

The woman nods. Pushes the knife slowly toward Chase.

It is the will of the Committee.

Thank you, Chase says, as Adam catches up to her. He looks at the knife on the table, at Chase.

You're not doing this alone!

In the wide Pit twenty feet from them a flame appears. It gushes forth, rising almost to the level of the topmost layer of blackened stone of the back wall of the Pit.

The child cries and cries.

Unable to stand it any longer, Chase scoops up the hunting knife from the table, stalks toward the roaring fire.

Adam follows. She turns on him.

No, Adam! You can't go with me.

In the midst of shadows cast by the flames one shadow moves, takes shape.

We drowned in the river, Adam says. I'm as dead as you are,

Chase! Maybe this place will be our Eternity. I don't care! As long as we're together.

Finally seed it my way, did ye, missy?

Chase whirls back toward the Pit, the flames. Crow stands there. The shadow he casts is in the shape of a dog, with disembodied but dazzling yellow-green eyes.

Adam puts a hand on Chase's arm. She shrugs him away. To Crow she screams, Where is he, you son of a bitch!

Wantin to see your firstborn?

I gave him away! I had to! Because he only would have reminded me of *you!*

Crow takes a couple of steps toward Chase and Adam, tilts his hat to the side of his head where most of the damage was done by the mushrooming slug from the Desert Eagle. There is a trickle of fresh blood, agleam in the firelight, down to his shirt collar. Crow puts an index finger into the gaping wound in a mock gesture of shooting himself all over again. He smiles.

Well now. Don't think ye be tellin the unvarnished truth, missy. Air ye? So ye gave him away—but it hurt ye to do it. Oh, it did. Ye was a good little mother whilst ye had him.

THE DANCE GOES ON

Hectic fiddles, shuffle of bodies in opposite circles.

Ladies to the left, gents to the right! Now choose 'nother partner and we'll dance all night!

WHILE AT THE PIT

Crow taunts Chase.

Ye always had fondness in your heart for your firstborn. Never mind as how I was its pappy. That did rankle me some.

The child wails.

Take me to him!

Surely. Right this way, missy. If ye dare.

CAMERA IS HIGH AND TURNING 360 DEGREES AS

Crow turns, walks down into the Pit and through the fire. Which erupts in a violent fountain of sparks, treetop high.

CHASE PLUNGES AFTER HIM, KNIFE IN HAND

BEHIND THEM ADAM CRIES OUT

Then Adam starts after Chase. But the shadow dog moves into his path, little more than glowing eyes and bared teeth.

Near Adam the members of the Committee rise slowly in solemn accord. Mute and gray as mummies, they stand watch. Sensing their interest, Adam turns to them.

Help me! I have to get to Chase! He'll destroy her!

But they neither move nor speak.

The shadow dog snarls at Adam's slightest move.

ON THE DANCE FLOOR

A fiddler glances at the sky and his bow falls trembling from taut strings. One by one the other musicians lose their place, stop playing, look up. The dancers shuffle and stall. All eyes are on the gourd-yellow moon.

THE MOON—THEIR POV

Thin clouds encircle it like streams of black ink jetted into the firmament. Tentacles that suck gluttonously the moon's pure light. A lamentation rises from the throats of the dancers. Then there is silence. They look around unwillingly, steeping themselves in one another's dread.

Once again the piercing wail of Chase's firstborn is heard.

A MEADOW

A place of misted lambency. No apparent end, no visible beginning. As if sealed in a dream. But the dream has a lurking margin of menace: a single, massive, gnarled oak tree stands black against the pearl sky, a drear reminder of Paradise dishonored.

In the floating mist there is a sudden spurt of flame, scintillant, like a fire medusa welling in a dimension of many-faceted crystals. In this preternatural world the wraith of Chase Emrick appears, comes forth humanly into the lovely dangerous meadow.

Crow Tillman is there, standing between her and a child's crib, its sides draped with blankets. He is looking back at Chase with a crooked smile of delight.

The cry of the unseen child has dwindled to a hurt, lost whimpering.

Chase's face is a study in desolation and yearning as she draws near the crib, almost unmindful of Crow.

Ain't it too bad what can happen when they's jest old nuff to toddle, and they gets too close to the edge of the highway?

From the crib a bloody hand reaches up to Chase.

She recoils in horror as Crow walks up behind her. Her hands go to her face and she sobs heartbrokenly.

Yeah, a reallll shame, Crow says, the rattlesnake hand gripping Chase's shoulder.

In a fury Chase turns. With the hunting knife and with strength doubled by grief, she cuts his left hand off at the wrist.

WE SEE THE HAND WITH THE RATTLESNAKE TATTOO

Lying in the meadow. Fingers move a little. Trickle of blood.

BEFORE CHASE CAN DELIVER ANOTHER STRIKE AT CROW WITH THE KNIFE

Her eyelids snap shut.

Chase slashes futilely at Crow as he nimbly dodges her, then steps in and smacks her hard on the jaw with his right hand.

Chase goes flying, losing her grip on the knife. Rolling over, she searches blindly for it in the blurred violet of the meadow while Crow stalks her, kicks her, pins her down with the sole and heel of a boot crushing her throat.

I done took em *all* away from ye, missy! Ever' last one ye held dear to your heart. They's only you left now.

Crow turns his head and whistles sharply to his black dog.

AT THE BARBECUE PIT

The shadow dog hears Crow's summoning whistle. It retreats from Adam's path until all that is seen of it are two glaring eyes.

Adam stares apprehensively at the high flames in the open Pit. Until he hears Chase scream.

Then he plunges down into the Pit and into the fire.

ON THE MEADOW

There is another manifestation, crystal starburst, and Adam comes through.

Crow Tillman casts a lazy eye on him, then rolls Chase over into reddish sedge with another savage kick.

As Chase cries out in pain Adam charges Crow with a vengeful scream.

Crow grins. Looks down.

THE TATTOOED RATTLESNAKE ON THE BACK OF
THE SEVERED HAND

Comes to life, uncoiling hugely to intercept Adam.

Adam is struck in midleap toward Crow. Struck in the face, he is driven back across the meadow by the power of the snake's vibrating tail until he strikes the black tree.

The long fangs of the serpent pin Adam to the trunk of the tree through his face and skull. Rattlesnake venom drips from Adam's chin as he screams again, in agony and terror.

CROW LOOKS AROUND TO ENJOY THE SHOW

Adam's body writhing, hands flailing, while all but the skull and fangs of the snake framing his face disappear as if they are soluble in the rising mist around the stark and twisted tree.

CHASE IS GALVANIZED BY ADAM'S SCREAMS

In spite of pain from cracked ribs she resumes pawing the meadow's turf in search of the dropped knife.

But Crow casually picks it up.

CLOSE ON THE MIRROR-FINISH BLADE

That reflects the moon as he turns the knife over in his hand.

THE MOON ITSELF

Is all grayish eyes in otherwise lifeless devastation. Hovering beside the moon is a massive, fulminating cloud, darker than the indigo of deep space.

AS FOR CROW AND CHASE:

He resumes his cruel taunting.

Reckon ye need to get acquainted with my rules. They's three things I don't never put up with in my woman. Which your Mama didn't pay heed to, much to her sorrow.

Punctuating this with another kick that rolls Chase over onto her back, gasping for breath before heaving out a word of contempt.

FUCKKKERRR!

Right. Talkin back be one a them things.

Now he prods Chase with the sharp toe of a boot, rolling her rag doll–style across the fuming meadow to a shallow sedgy pool. She is unable to resist him any longer.

No. Reckon that be all three a my rules. In a nutshell. Don't talk back. No time, nowheres, nohow. We got ourselves a bargain?

Chase groans, fingers prying futilely at her stuck eyelids.

Let's jest seal our bargain with a kiss. Honey.

CROW SETS THE BLADE OF THE KNIFE BETWEEN HIS TEETH

The sharp edge out. He reaches down and hauls Chase to her feet.

Then he notices something strange to his senses. He gives Chase a hard shake to make her hold still in his grasp and looks around.

There is a wind upon the meadow. The mist is in motion. And the bare crooked limbs of the tree upon which Adam is now laxly impaled are moving.

The brightness of the moon has dimmed.

While Crow is distracted by these changes in a normally changeless place Chase's hands are busy. One of them closes on his thick wrist. She pushes against the hand that holds her by her blouse and gains a bit of leverage.

Her other hand finds the handle of the knife he is holding between his teeth.

Sightlessly informing herself of his position and the angle of his arm by the hold she has on him, Chase yanks the knife from between Crow's teeth and sinks the blade at a downward angle into his solar plexus.

Shocked by the cold thrust of the blade, Crow lets go of Chase. She drops to her knees and scrambles backward. Feeling a gush of black wind in her face as if a door has been opened on a cyclone.

Crow looks down, then touches the staghorn haft of the

knife canted solidly against his chest wall. All of the blade seated inside him.

Got a fast pair a hands, ain't ye? Right through the heart, missy. If 'n I had one. Which I don't.

Crow laughs. And tries to pull the knife from his chest. Chase rises unsteadily, turning away from the careering wind with a steadily rising velocity and the high keen of a train whistle.

The knife won't budge as Crow tugs at it.

Puzzled, Crow tries harder. The down-flowing wind from that mass of cloud overwhelming the sky picks his hat off his head and spirits it away.

Damn ye! Crow screams at Chase. Where'd ye go? He is half blinded himself from tears in his sighted eye. Come and he'p me get this blade unstuck ye little bitch!

Chase backs away, head down into the wind, a smile beginning on her face, for there is fear in Crow's voice. If only she could see him now.

Ye can't do this to me!

Chase keeps moving off from him, now guided in her blind faltering steps by a network of exposed far-spread roots to the gnarled tree with a trunk as thick as a silo.

Crow's voice, cursing her, grows fainter in the shrill wind.

Crow looks away from the retreating Chase. Looks up at approaching darkness. A whiplash of cosmic debris sets him to howling and flinching. But he remains, defiantly, on his feet.

Ain't goin nowheres! And ye ain't never gettin rid a me, Chase Emrick!

He hazards a look at her as

CHASE FINDS THE RELATIVE SAFETY OF THE TREE

Pressing back into a deep cleft not far from where Adam is hung, his body moving only in response to the whipping wind. Within her modest sanctuary Chase doesn't know he is there—

AND CROW

—Has the black eye patch peeled from his head.

The intagliated lightning-crawl of his glass eye flares deeply.

Then, glowing like an ingot, the lightning expands. It runs lividly beneath the skin of his face and neck, spreading across the chest wall to make contact with the hilt of the huntsman's knife.

CHASE'S EYELIDS SPRING OPEN AS

CHASE'S POV

She sees Crow Tillman electrified in shocking relief against the surging black cloud. His body is shot through and through with an intense pulsating light that combusts all flesh, turns his standing bones to an armature painted with eternal fire.

Then, as if by the flourish of a magician's great black cloak, what remains of Crow is swept up and vanishes from her sight.

CHASE

Edges unsteadily out of the cleft of the tree, nauseated, deafened, her lungs struggling to move in her breast. They feel as heavy as sunken sacks of treasure. She shudders as if an icy current swirls around her. The black cloud has left the meadow as timelessly composed as ever. The child's crib also is gone.

And her firstborn. Whom she senses, with a twinge of relief, now lives again, far from the Netherworld. Lives contentedly, free of any taint of his paternal bloodline.

She moves haltingly to her right, where a dangling hand brushes her cheek.

ADAM!

Chase clings to him, struggling to loosen his inert body from the cage of fangs holding him spike-fast to the trunk of the tree.

The cold grip of an element denser than air is stronger than the hold Chase has on her lover, on his spectral remains death-glowing in the full cleansing light of the moon on the now-remote meadow. She hears the distant booming of her, or someone's, ponderous heart.

Please you have to come with me!

But she is losing Adam—losing herself at the precarious threshold to the past, a past she is desperate not to reenter if he won't be there.

PleasePLEASE sweet angel!

(So cold.)

The pressure outside her body, the pressure within. *I can't! It's so unfair. I don't want to be alone!*

(Her numbed hand slipping from his.)

Her weighted lungs an impossible burden, a barrier she cannot pass. But she doesn't want to. Not this time.

Adrift. Listening. Hearing the hollow booming of a heart in a dark cavern.

The balky engine of her long-stalled heart.

Cold.

(. . . oh adam . . .)

Chase
May. This Year.

Hello, Adam! Sorry I'm late this morning. I mean it's not all *that* late. Twenty minutes to nine.

———————————

Because it's Tuesday I have an eleven o'clock class in Euclidian—but that gives us, let's see, almost two hours together.

———————————

It's a beautiful morning. The azaleas and rhodies on campus are finally in full bloom, along with all the dogwoods. After all the rain we've had it's a chance, for the next three days according to the weatherman, to get out and walk. I'm past the stage where I can bike comfortably. Rollerblades, uh-uh. Dr. Huffman let me do pretty much whatever I was comfortable with the first six months, but now that we're getting serious about having our baby—three months to go, can you believe it?—I need to be a little more cautious for Adam Jr.'s sake. Treadmill's still okay. The news is he's *very* active. Wakes me up a couple of times a night. But that's okay, usually I need to get up anyway and pee.

But I guess I already told you that yesterday. About our son. I know I talk about him a lot and he's not even here yet. Can't help it. I get so excited—I'm not the only one. Your mom's been calling every day. Or night, depending on where she is. Kyoto. Santiago. Belgium, this week. She's overseeing the installation of some of her work at the exhibit in Ghent. The little stuff, that five strong men can lift. You know about that. Anyway it's kind of amazing how close we've become after a really bad start. But you were there. What I mean is, she's creative, and I'm—well, creative in my own field. In a way that maybe fifty people in the world can understand. Begin to understand. Want to.

Your mother has a lot to say about what you were like, when I prod her to open up. Remember. Stuff I really—I'm kind of desperate to know, because we had such a short time together, almost no time really to—I'd like to say *get acquainted*, because—it's funny now—how fast we were in bed together the first time, not knowing anything about each other except what I saw—in your eyes. My eyes, sure; after all you picked me up, didn't you? Literally picked me up when—I pass on your mother's stories to Adam Jr. late at night when it's just the two of us, he's kicking away and I can't fall asleep and TV's mostly infomercials and I—I ache so much from missing you.

Okay, there I go. Such a gorgeous day and I have to get weepy. Sorry.

Probably Sergei or Linda or maybe both will stop by in a little while. I called and told them I'd be here this morning, and not this afternoon: there's a Master's Tea at four o'clock at JE I scored a ticket for. They've invited the French philosopher Jean Beaudrillard. Sergei may already have seen you, first thing today. And I know how busy they keep you, with therapy, so that when you—you've come back to us, there's every chance that eventually you'll be a hundred percent physically. It was a couple of weeks before I could walk again, and I "came back" in less than a month. But we have to be—you know. Realistic about your own recovery period.

And I know it's going to happen! You *will* come back to us. I know that Sergei and Linda and all of the neurological consultants who have been in and out of here are—not as positive as I am, but if Adam Jr. and I both made it—Adam, I'm saying—I'm telling you that we need you. And damn it, we will *never* give up!

Chase
June. This Year.
The Summer Solstice.

I spent part of the day that Adam came back to us having lunch in New York with Stella at the Yale Club. She also wanted to shop for Adam Junior, at a far-too-pricey boutique a few blocks away on Lexington. But she is a woman of means and Adam Junior's grandmother so I kept quiet, smiled a lot, and let her do the choosing in infants' wear. I thought she had excellent taste. And she'd had three children herself.

"Promise me one thing," Stella said. "Do not let ANYONE on your side of the family ever refer to me as 'Mamaw.'" She shuddered at the horror of it.

"Not too many left on my side of the family," I said.

"Chase, are you getting enough rest?" she said with a critical look at the puffiness under my eyes. "At this stage of your pregnancy you ought to be RADIANT. I know I was."

"I try," I said, feeling drab and outclassed by Stell's celebrity panache.

"Now, I've heard from a couple of the nurses on Adam's team that they sometimes find you asleep in a chair by his bed, as late as two in the morning."

"I just feel," I said, thinking it over as I spoke, "there are times when he wants me with him more than at other times. I can't account for that rationally. It's like a psychic tickle, a blood urgency. A kind of, of *knowing*."

"Well," she said, nodding, "I don't disdain the paranormal. Although Sun Lin's father, who otherwise was a brilliant set designer, took his mystic bent too far. He would consult at least three horoscopes before settling into bed for the night. Sidereal, Vedic, Chinese, even the sort of rubbish they publish in the *Post* next to the funnies. He was born in the Year of the Dog, for what that's worth. Now then. Your first responsibility is to the baby. Which means of course taking care of your-SELF. Tomato aspic and a few nibbles of lettuce does not constitute a suitably nourishing lunch."

"I feel fat, Stella. I know it's okay to gain weight. I have a big frame. Dr. Huffman says I can easily handle an extra twenty-five pounds. But—"

"We'll talk further about that," Stella said, adding my fat-neurosis to her mental list of Things We Were Going to Discuss eventually. "But let's get to why I really wanted to see you today."

"Okay."

"First of all, I was wondering if it was really necessary for you to shoulder another teaching load during the Summer session? The pay is not all that much."

"Teaching keeps me occupied."

"But what is your first responsibility as your time grows near?"

"The baby."

"Yes. You've been under a double strain. Long hours at the Frohlinger, bills to pay. It's emotionally draining. You need to step back, take a breath, accept—"

She was alert to the warning in my eyes, and veered away from the subject of Adam's prognosis.

"What I wish to say, at my discretion the terms of Adam's major trust—his father by the way, died intestate, spending his last dime on the way to the grave—the terms can be restructured so as to provide you and Adam Junior with a significant monthly income—"

"Until Adam recovers."

"Yes. Of course," Stella said, eyes downcast for a few moments, a little stitch at one corner of her taut mouth. I knew that she had given up hope for Adam as soon as she saw him connected *in extremis* to all that tubing in his twilight bed. Probably she hadn't thought much of my chances either, although only a few hours after divers pulled us out of the Saugatuck River, twenty minutes after we drowned in thirty-seven-degree waters, I showed activity in the higher-order cognitive regions of the brain. Three weeks later, responding to hyperbaric treatments, I was up and taking baby steps. All thanks to Sergei Olanovsky. Written up in papers worldwide. Turning down pleas from Oprah and Katie and Barbara to explain my miraculous recovery, for a second time, on national TV.

But Adam remained vegatative, not opening his eyes. And I just wanted to be left alone.

Over cups of honey-sweetened white tea Stella resumed where she had left off.

"I've come to know you well enough to be assured you won't be spoiled by money. You have a brilliant mind which you'll continue to put to good use. Nor am I about to try to run your life."

"I know, Stella."

"But."

I sipped my tea and smiled disarmingly.

"But I do think it would greatly benefit you to get away for two or three weeks where all of your needs will be taken care of. I'm talking *pampered*. While you have a daily swim in your pool, sit on your terrace, and gaze at the sea."

"Where is all this happening, Stell?"

She had a folder of photographs with her, and eagerly began handing them to me one at a time. I looked at views of a trim one-story stone villa on a hillside surrounded by splashy purple bougainvillea and Mediterranean cypress.

"It's in the south of France. Golfe-Juan. I took it over from a cousin of mine who got in a financial jam a few years ago. But I seldom have the chance to use it. Fully staffed, of course. There's nowhere more relaxing than Provence, even in high summer, as long as you steer clear of the mobs in Nice or Cannes."

I looked at the photos and didn't say anything. But my feelings were plain enough, I guess.

"Now don't be an idiot," Stella said sharply. "There has been no change in the neural images of my son, your husband, for months now." She stopped short of saying *and there never will be.* "You don't have to be at his side for hours every day no matter what psychic currents you're feeling. Get away, Chase. If there should be the slightest improvement you'll be told immediately. Meanwhile—"

Stella looked at her watch, and signaled a waiter.

"We're due at my lawyer's at three o'clock. To sign papers."

"What papers?"

"Whatever you decide about a retreat, I'm deeding the villa to you, in trust for Adam Junior. Someday you may appreciate me for doing this."

She smiled curtly, blinking. The sudden annoyance of tears. She turned her face away. I reached across the table and held her hand.

"I love you, Stell," I said.

✤

On the train back to New Haven I had an episode of EBS that lasted roughly the time it took to get from Norwalk to Westport, about three minutes. My eyes opened shortly after we left the Westport station and were rolling across the river.

Looking down from the bridge I had an eerie hallucination, as if I saw Adam's old orange Datsun submerged just below the surface as the tide was going out. It shook me badly. Talk about psychic currents. And when I looked away and at the seat opposite me I was jolted again. It was only a teenage boy but uncannily he had Adam's face. He was listening to his iPod and staring at me.

"Fall asleep?" he said with a smile.

I took a cab from Union Station to the Frohlinger Institute, a fifteen-minute ride to the campus near Hampden. When I got there I felt as if I'd been holding my breath most of the way. Feeling a little dazed, anxious, hopeful.

But when I reached the "clean room" in which Adam had lain comatose for a little more than five months, connected to white tubing as thick as my wrist, there was no change. A nasal canula assisted his breathing. One glance at the neural imaging screen told me a familiar story. Very little preserved function in isolated brain areas. That had been a constant since he was pulled from the river and resuscitation began.

As I stared unseeingly at the face of a vital-signs monitor, barely aware of my own ghostly reflection, the monitor beeped. A peak that seemed like a stiletto compared to the mildly saw-toothed undulant line that had appeared across the screen. A moment later there was another.

"Adam?"

I could almost feel the draining of blood from my head. I took several steps toward the bed feeling slow, awkward, disbelieving. But the monitor continued to beep every three or four seconds.

"Adam, it's Chase!"

I know I screamed it, wild with joy. I was already beginning to faint from light-headedness when two LPNs ran into the isolation room and grabbed me.

By then I had seen his eyes wide open. He appeared to stare right at me. That was all I could recall, just then, of his face with the healed puncture wounds, the rivulets of scars where snake's venom had drained.

They helped me from the room. I was sobbing, near-hysterical.

I saw Sergei Olanovsky at the nursing station, his head turning toward me. I made an effort to regain control of myself, broke free of the helping hands, ran to him.

"What is it, Chase?"

"He's coming back!"

Sergei put both arms around me; otherwise I might have collapsed again before I had the chance to tell him what I'd seen. What he must do.

"KILL HIM. KILL him *now*, Sergei! Pull all the plugs, make him die!"

He jerked his head back in amazement.

"What do you mean? What are you saying?"

"His eyes opened! I saw his eyes! Oh, God, please listen to me! For my sake, for the sake of my baby—KILL HIM! He's coming back, *but he isn't Adam anymore*!

Chase
Three Years Later.

Therese is clearing the table on the terrace and the long Provençal dusk is beginning, the air cooling slightly. Therese's husband, Marcel, who cooks for us, is Corsican. We ate lightly as we always do on summer evenings: tossed salad, a *ficatellu*, or kid ragout (which was always Stella's favorite when she came to visit), and Corsican polenta made from chestnut flour.

Across Golfe Juan the light on the cape at Eden Roc is flashing now, visible along with a few stars in the southern sky and the lights of a small cruise ship outbound from Cannes. The sea is calm, deep blue.

Dory called this afternoon from Prague. She'll only be in Paris for a day instead of the four she had planned. So a quick visit to see Casey and me appears out of the question. She asked me to fly to Paris for a few hours but I told her that Case was getting over a summer cold. Anyway, Dory knows I don't leave my son with anyone, not even the conscientious Therese, for so much as an hour, let alone a full day.

I have a tote filled with downloaded abstracts, queries from colleagues and a ninety-six page draft of my theorem beside my chair, but work is far from my mind.

Casey's playing croquet on the lawn with his friends Andre and Dominique from the villa next door. Dominique is older than the boys, and bossy, but Case gives it right back to her, scolding in French. Although he won't be three until September, already he has a bigger vocabulary than I do. But I'm tone-deaf and have no head for languages.

The bodyguard of Andre and Dominique is nearby, in a lawn swing sipping coffee Therese carried to him. Their father is some sort of financier—venture capital, hedge funds—and is worth a mint. So that's how it is down here. The Côte d'Azur is lovely. The Côte is also a magnet for thieves and worse. You watch your kids very closely.

But I won't let Casey go to Andre's to play in spite of the walls, the brute dogs, the alarms. Not unless I'm with him.

We have three macaws in cages on the terrace: a gnarly-looking military and two Hyacinthines as blue as the sea. They're as observant as watchdogs. Until recently we had a Lahsa Apso named Baba. She was a feisty descendant of Tibetan temple dogs. Devoted to Casey. She slept at the foot of his bed. But Baba was killed in the yard by a marauder of some kind.

Coyote, Marcel said. But I knew better.

✦

Stella is dead.

In her workshop in the old brewery building in Brooklyn. One of her workbenches fell over on her and crushed her chest. That was the best explanation they could come up with—the detectives who investigated. A solid maple workbench weighing upward of three hundred pounds just fell over on her.

But I knew better.

Stella Moritz had become my friend and ally in my most difficult times following Casey's birth. So she had to go.

All I have left is Casey.

It's getting a little too dark now for more playtime. In a few minutes I'll call him up to the terrace, bring him closer, hold him in my lap while we spend half an hour or so on his math flash cards.

A month ago Adam took his first steps at the Frohlinger. He's still hampered by the paralysis on his right side, but that seems slowly to be improving. He's also begun to say a few words.

In the CDs Dory sends for Casey and me to watch on our computer he smiles often. His eyes are clear and bright.

There is no sign of the lightning gash in the sightless right eye that I saw when he looked at me for the first time after his drowning in the isolation room at the Frohlinger.

No one else assigned to his case has ever admitted seeing it too.

Maybe they haven't. But it was there, had been there, if only for a few moments.

Long enough for me to *know*.

"Qui est l'homme?" Casey asked me, the first time we looked at one of the CDs.

"He's your father, Casey."

"Is he sick, Mama?"

"Yes. Very sick."

"Is that why he doesn't live with us?"

"Yes," I said.

I tried twice to kill Adam myself, once before Casey was born and again a few months later. Each time I wasn't alone with Adam quite long enough.

The second time they blamed it on postpartum depression. But I was never allowed to be alone with him again, and soon I stopped going to see him.

Sergei, Dory—they all wonder why. He is my husband. He's made a remarkable recovery.

Why don't you come to see him, Chase?

Because I don't have to.

He comes to me.

To us.

In another half hour it will be full dark. The tree frogs are in doleful chorus. A twinkling jet slides past the moon on its approach to the airport at Nice. Casey will be asleep in my lap smelling of summer and hard play, and I'll gently pry his thumb from his mouth. He's getting too big for that. I'll be listening to Garth Brooks or Trisha Yearwood on my iPod.

Gazing out over the sloping lawn with its outcrops of stone to the sea.

Waiting.

*

It doesn't come around every night. A week might go by, and there is no visitation.

But night will fall, and I will hold Casey close to me, and then I'll see it: bounding up the moon-silvered lawn, then slowing near the terrace and circling in a prowl, so softly that even the macaws in their cages are not disturbed.

Each time it appears it dares to come a little closer—yellow-green eyes afire. It sits patiently outside the moon gate in the cornered remnant of the west wall of the terrace. Its tongue lolls. It stares at me and the most precious thing I have, his small heart beating slowly against my breast. My child. Cuddled, protected.

*

(What was love became hate. But I have survived both. I am strong.)

Yet I feel the growing strength of the black dog's fetch.

Black dog. Black dog. Familiar haunter. You have all of your victims but one. You will never have him. Because you don't scare me.

You don't scare me.